ANDY IVEY

Castle Gap

A Chase Haven Thriller

to the warrior who painted the house like a skunk

Contents

1

The Butterfield

"You know the people of our town are too stupid to understand the airport!" That was the shrill voice of a screaming Turner Cam. Chase could tell he was bright red, a terribly unnatural shade, even from behind.

The entire room was frozen in shock. Chase Haven was too. He was stuck, wide-eyed, half-in and half-out of the doorway. He could see through the large windows that everyone was standing. He had walked in off the street assuming the meeting was over. Instead, he was a witness to the outburst.

Moments earlier, Chase had been sitting at the bar of the Butterfield lost in a daydream he couldn't later recall. The frosty glass in his hand was cold, too cold to hold comfortably. He didn't notice the pleas from his fingers to retreat. He stared blankly at the polished finish of the bar, a silent witness to history and a relic of a bygone era. It bore the marks of countless travelers to the town's abandoned railway station from which it had been rescued.

A loud slap of a hand against the wooden bar brought him out of his daydream. His head turned toward the sound while he simultaneously withdrew his hand, now tingling from the cold. It was the smiling face of Stefan Beldame, who was trailed by his wife, Corely.

Before he or his friends had a chance to exchange hellos, they were interrupted by Hayden Mulvaney who stood behind the bar. "Hey, guys! What can I get ya?"

"We just needed a break from the chaos. The usual for both of us," Corely said.

"Two chicken frieds. Coming right up."

"Not even a menu for these two," Chase said. He stood and gave Corely a hug before shaking Stefan's hand. They each sat on stools lined three across. Behind them were the many four-top tables that made up the restaurant area of the Butterfield. There was no doubt the couple had stopped at every table on their way in and exchanged greetings with every local.

"Work's been relentless lately. Plus, I've got some news," Stefan said, turning toward Chase.

"Spill it."

"We're on an adventure tonight," Corely said.

"We got ourselves an appointment to see your girlfriend," Stefan added.

"Tacy? You sure? She said she had an EDC meet—"

"Our meeting. We got ourselves appointed to the board," Corely said.

"Gluttons for punishment, I see," Chase replied. Laughs all around.

"You know the Grahams?" Corely asked. It sounded more like a statement than a question.

"You bet; they used to own the title company," Chase said. The title company had changed hands long before Chase moved to town, and he was proud to show he knew what was going on.

"We're taking their spots on the board. They rolled off. The Grahams said they just rubber-stamp everything, but it is a good way to get involved," Corely said.

"Rubber-stamp? Tacy said they're voting on expanding the airport tonight."

"The mayor and city manager want our board to sign a loan for it. No big deal," Stefan said.

"Hmmm. You know what they say about needing someone to cosign your loan?" Chase replied, a sly smile beginning to appear across his face.

"No. What?" Corely asked.

"If you need a cosigner, you can't afford it."

"Funny," she said, but didn't laugh. "What *can* we afford? The city doesn't have any money."

Chase knew that to be true just by looking around the aging town. However, Stefan had joked that the town of three thousand could unleash the resources of a city five times its size, but only if a powerful family chose to put their name and resources behind the initiative. Chase had not yet seen that in action.

The three friends were quickly drawn into everyday conversation. Occasionally they were joined by the friendly Hayden and a few other local faces. The bar could be completely empty or standing room only on any given night. A high school basketball game or a church supper could siphon off every last customer with little notice.

It wasn't long before the Beldames said goodbye and left the Butterfield for the short walk across the town square. Chase had planned to sit tight and order some food, but he instead chose to catch what he hoped was the end of Tacy's meeting.

Chase figured the meeting might last an hour and timed his

last beer and the walk to get him there. The entire square was dark. Most storefronts were vacant or home to an insurance agency or real estate office that closed by 5 p.m. The lone light on the far side of the square was coming through the large glass windows of the Chamber of Commerce, where Tacy held her meeting.

It looked like the meeting had ended as Chase put his hand on the door. Everyone was standing and looking at Turner Cam, who stood in the audience. The mayor was ever-present at every function in town. He dressed in a steady rotation of polo shirts, casual slacks, and white tennis shoes. He was speaking loudly, but Chase couldn't make out the words until he opened the door.

Ding. The door chimed noisily as it opened, but no one looked toward Chase. That's when he was hit by the mayor's outburst.

"You know the people of our town are too stupid to understand the airport!"

Corely shot a silent "*What!?*" to her husband that was visible from across the room. The rest of the board, all seasoned business leaders in the small community of Horsehead Crossing, Texas, quietly walked to a back room in the building. Not a comment.

The board members were followed by Tacy, who had been sitting in the audience with her back to Chase. She was the lone employee of the Economic Development Corporation, a.k.a. the EDC. Her job was to run the day-to-day of an organization that mostly gave local businesses small grants for new signage or a piece of equipment. Her job tonight was to stream the meeting online to a Facebook audience of probably zero.

Chase was wrong about the meeting being over. The board was instead deliberating something in private. He stepped into the room and let the door close behind him. It shut with a metal-on-metal clang that stiffened his joints. Thankfully, the mayor didn't turn towards the noise.

Instead, Turner Cam took a seat next to the only other person left in the room, City Manager Aaron Foster. The city manager was not ever-present. If he was seen in town, he was always in a suit or slacks or some professional attire. There was usually a tie, and it wasn't a fun one. No trendy or novelty ties for Mr. Foster. If he spoke, he used words like he had only been given so many for one lifetime and he didn't want to run out.

Chase nervously took a seat in the back row. He was thankful neither man acknowledged his presence beyond shooting him a lone glance over their shoulders. Hushed words were spoken between them that Chase couldn't make out.

After twenty minutes, during which Chase mostly looked at his phone, the board returned to the room. They assembled in silence before their chairman restarted the meeting.

There was no discussion. The group voted 3-2 against cosigning the loan for the airport and then adjourned. Stefan and Corely voted against the project. They were joined by Brady Laye, who processed deer during hunting season and cattle, sheep, goats, and pigs for the local ranchers at Laye Texas Meats.

The mayor sprung from his seat and extended his hand to the nearest board member. "I really just want to thank you for your service," he said. The mayor always struck Chase as sickly sweet. It was gross. Kindness dripped from him as he acted as if his earlier outburst never occurred.

He repeated this with every board member, who joined him in the act of pretending he hadn't just had an insane outburst. Even Stefan acted like everything was normal, but

5

Corely couldn't shake a bewildered look from her face. "You're welcome," she said.

Aaron Foster left the meeting with his head down. He didn't look toward Chase again. Turner Cam did, though. He glared, actually. Chase couldn't help but return an involuntary scowl as Turner left the building.

Still looking angrily through the window in the direction of the mayor, Chase felt a tug on his arm. He swore he smelled her before he saw her. Tacy, the young, former college breakaway roper, made him nervous each time he saw her.

The smell. It was sweet like mint. Spicy actually. He hadn't had his own word for that smell. Cardamom. That's what she called it.

He gave her a hug, which did nothing to erase the look of stress on her face. "Interesting meeting," Chase said. He wasn't sure if it was a statement or a question.

"That's the first time we've ever voted anything down," Tacy said.

Stefan and Corely joined them as the rest of the board filed out quietly.

"What was that about?" Corely asked.

"I don't think the mayor liked being questioned. He definitely wouldn't have liked how it went in closed session. We called the city attorney, and he didn't seem to understand the project any more than we did," Stefan said.

"I don't know if those two have ever been told no before," Tacy said. She still clung to Chase's arm. "We wouldn't have had that third vote if the mayor hadn't yelled at everyone for suggesting that the city borrow the money itself."

"The airport doesn't even make money," Stefan said.

"Then why are they pushing it so hard?" Chase asked.

"I don't know," Corely replied. She turned toward the door. The group followed suit.

"Just a rubber stamp, huh?" Chase asked, looking over at Stefan and offering a sly smile.

Stefan shrugged. "Yeah, just a rubber stamp."

"And why'd he thank us?" Corely asked.

"That man is what you call the south end of a northbound horse," Tacy said.

2

X in Texas

"You treat us like a piggy bank," Brady Laye said. He was mid-conversation, standing next to his pickup with the open door between him and Turner Cam.

This is the sight that greeted the friends when they flipped off the lights and opened the door of the Chamber of Commerce building. There was Tacy, holding Chase's hand, plus Corely and Stefan—four unintended witnesses to an argument. They were in earshot of the two men, who did not turn toward them as the door chimed open.

Brady continued, "I wouldn't sign the loan if it was my business with those financials."

"You should have gone to Aaron and asked him questions in his office. When that young thing in there spoke up and said the city could take out the loan itself, she was out of line. She's just an employee. You are a board member. You let her steer you," Turner said. He was red, although not the crimson shade of earlier.

Chase squeezed Tacy's hand, and she shot him a puzzled look. None of the group moved, much less made a sound.

"We all just need to take a step back for a second. You can still get what you want," Brady said. He rested his hands on the inside of the truck door.

Turner continued at a much lower volume. "This is too complicated to discuss in a public meeting. There's a lot going on here. You should have told Aaron you had concerns." He took a step back. "If you wanted to see more details about the project, you had to vote for it so we could get bids to build it. Aaron could have explained that."

The two stood in silence for a moment before Turner spoke again. "Decisions have consequences, Brady." He then turned and crossed the square towards city hall.

"What does that mean!?" Brady yelled. Turner never looked back. He never looked in the direction of the four onlookers who stood in the doorway of the darkened building.

Brady sat in his truck but made no effort to close the door. He stared through his windshield. It felt like forever before he spotted the group. Once he did, and there was no mistaking that he had, he quickly fired up his truck and drove off.

"You steered us?" Stefan asked. He was the first to speak.

"How?" Tacy asked. "Brady asked Aaron and Turner if they could fund the project any other way and they didn't answer. I was just trying to help."

"You didn't steer anybody," Corely said. "Don't worry about it. Let's get out of here. How about a late dinner at our place?"

"Didn't you two already eat?" Chase asked.

"We can eat again. Come on," Corely replied. She grabbed Tacy, who was still holding Chase's hand, and pulled them both towards the Butterfield where they were parked.

"She can ride with me, if she wants," Chase said. He wrapped his arm around Tacy's shoulder. She leaned into him.

Tacy didn't speak during their short drive to the Beldames' hobby ranch. Chase didn't interrupt her thoughts. He was just happy that she had scooted across the bench seat and leaned against him as he drove.

Cardamom. That's what she called it.

Like many homesteads on the edge of town, the couple's small acreage had been carved from a larger ranch that still sat intact behind them. These properties were attractive to people that made frequent trips for their "town" jobs.

The town jobs for the Beldames involved selling ranches in Crane, Pecos, and Upton County. That's how they met Chase. They sold him his place and welcomed him to town as friends.

Stefan poked his head out of his front door as Tacy and Chase got out of the truck. "How about we heat up some *birria de res*? Corely made it yesterday. It's perfect. And, most expensive beef in Texas," Stefan said. "Most expensive beef in Texas" was a joke he repeated often. He and Corely raised just enough Hereford cattle to keep their freezers full of beef, but they had to buy hay all year, which made this hobby less than economical.

Once inside, Corely got busy at the stove heating a pot. The smell of garlic, onion, and chilies slowly filled the room. Stefan, who was obviously the assistant, appeared to be in charge of drinks and dishes.

Tacy and Chase sat at the kitchen bar watching the two work. The local newspaper sat folded on the counter in front of them.

"What's the newspaper going to say about all of this?" Chase asked.

"The newspaper? Nothing probably," Corely said.

"Should we go to them with the story?" Chase asked.

Stefan produced a bottle of red wine, a bottle opener, and some glasses, which he set in front of his guests. "Let me tell

10

you about the paper before you do anything."

He pulled a bottle of whiskey from a cabinet and paused as if he was presenting it to the pair. "My dad used to say that the old newspaper owner was buried under the X in Texas."

He looked to his two guests to see if the saying registered with them. "He disappeared one night. His house and the newspaper office were eventually foreclosed on and sold at auction."

Corely picked up the story. "A local family bought the newspaper building and a short time later we had a newspaper again."

"What family?" Chase asked.

"Baxter Whitey, as in Whitey Family Holdings. He owns half the town. Half the county," Corely said.

"And he killed the guy?" Chase asked.

"Or maybe he just ran him off. Or just took advantage of the situation. The old newspaper guy took the wrong side back when we were voting to go wet—to finally sell alcohol within the city limits. When the city council announced there'd be a vote on the topic, the newspaper published an article supporting the idea. That was all anyone talked about. They say that the owner of the paper started getting death threats," Stefan said.

Stefan produced bowls and silverware from various cabinets and drawers as they spoke.

"This controversy was all over beer?" Chase asked. He was working on opening the bottle of wine, something red.

"Yup. A lot of people wanted the area to stay dry. Anyway, the guy ended up vanishing one day."

"Oh. Wow. Okay. How do you buy a newspaper from a dead guy?" Tacy asked.

"Anything seems possible for Baxter Whitey. I guess when

you buy the building, you get the paper. Suddenly, we had a paper again, and his wife Rebecca was running the show."

"And Turner Cam was their top pick for mayor?" Tacy asked.

Corely set a bowl of stew in front of Tacy. Stefan followed behind with silverware and a napkin as he spoke. "Had to be. The newspaper turns a blind eye to all the election funny business in the city. Some people won't even vote because of Aaron and Turner. They'll walk around city hall while you vote and tell you who they think you should support. Some say they're looking over your shoulder."

A second bowl was delivered to Chase.

"I just never made a connection between those two and Baxter Whitey," Tacy said.

"Somebody from the city government is down at the news-paper almost every day. None of this election nonsense was ever mentioned. But, I guess all of that was before you two got here," Corely said.

The four sat around the kitchen island eating and drinking. Tacy recounted all of the projects that had come across her desk, starting when she was an intern at the EDC. After the previous director never returned from maternity leave, the job went to Tacy, and the projects kept coming.

"Where do the projects come from, Tacy?" Chase asked.

"If they came from city hall, they always got funded. Any big project we pitched ourselves always got lost," Tacy said.

"Lost?" Stefan asked.

"Yeah, we'd send it to the city attorney, and he'd just say it wasn't a priority. Once he did that, it wouldn't even appear on the agenda for discussion."

"What's the deal with that guy anyway?" Corely asked.

"The city attorney?" Tacy asked.

"Yeah, is his title so important that he makes people call him by it? Why don't people call him Steve or whatever his name is?"

Stefan interjected. "He's an NPC. You have a better chance of winning the lottery than seeing that man outside of a city council meeting. I don't know how that started, but it fits if you've been around him for any time. If you do somehow see him outside a city council meeting, he's sitting alone and never talking to anyone. Ever."

Corely held up her hand. "Hold on. What's an NPC?"

"Like in a computer game. A Non-Player Character or something. They're controlled by the game and can only do what they're programmed to do. He's 100 percent city attorney and 0 percent human."

3

City Email

Chase ordered his usual Americano and sat down in his regular seat, an oversized leather chair. The Butterfield, named after an 1850s stagecoach service that crossed the nearby Pecos River, doubled as the town everything. That included a coffee shop, which was tucked in one corner of the place and was run by Hayden's daughter.

Chase shouldn't have felt the need to order the more expensive espresso mixed with water instead of the cheaper drip coffee. He shouldn't have felt the need to justify taking up space in a chair each morning since they would otherwise sit unused. However, he did. That feeling drove his morning routine as much as anything.

The chime of the door and the high-pitched whine of the espresso machine were the only things to disrupt the quiet of the morning. Everyone was in a hurry to get to work or run kids to school except Chase. He was always the lone "here" order in a world of "to-go."

Signs on the walls, out of date now, reminded him that there had been a concert that past weekend. A local act played after the tables were cleared to produce a makeshift dance floor, the only one for miles. Tacy got him to dance on occasion, but she still hadn't fixed his two-step. He had shuffled around as best he could in an attempt to keep up with her.

The next ding of the door was Stefan Beldame. He took the matching leather chair directly across a small table that separated them.

"What's up, chicken rancher?" Stefan asked. He was eyeing a carton of eggs sitting next to Chase. "Restocking the shelves?"

Chase's job, one of them at least, was selling fresh eggs in a little countertop display at the Butterfield. His Americana hens were putting out more eggs than he would have been able to sell if it hadn't been for Hayden. He owed him for that. Hayden mentioned the eggs to everyone that walked in the door until the first batch was sold out. After that, repeat business took all Chase could stock.

He tapped the eggs and smiled as he replied, "Beer money."

"Very masculine." Stefan laughed.

"You know chickens came with the place. You were the guy that sold it to me."

"Yeah, I just didn't really think you'd turn it into a business."

"YouTube, man. There's nothing you can't learn on YouTube. Anyway, what's up?"

"Did your girlfriend head to work already?"

Chase shrugged. "I assume so. I haven't talked to her yet."

"Well, I assumed you were—"

"Yes?" Chase raised his eyebrows and leaned forward.

Stefan smiled. "Aren't you a good Boy Scout."

"I'm dating a good Lutheran girl. No funny business." He did not match Stefan's smile.

"I thought barrel racers were supposed to be wild."

"Breakaway roper. What do you need again?"

"I wanted to catch you before you go fistfight the mayor or whatever is on your schedule today."

"I've thought about it. I might have a little bit of a temper, sure, and if you ask me if I'm sleeping with Tacy ever again, I'm going to punch *you* instead." Chase finally smiled.

"I went by Laye Texas Meats on my way into town. Brady didn't have much to share, but he knows we saw him. I told him we'd keep our mouths shut. I just wanted to get that message to you and Tacy."

"Tacy said she was going to put together all the projects the city killed. There are three or four big ones she thinks were shut down by the city attorney."

The two looked to the door as it chimed. It was Corely. She made a beeline to them.

"Hey, we just got an email," Corely said.

"We?" Stefan asked.

"You and me. From Aaron Foster."

"Oh, okay . . ."

"It's . . . not good." She looked to Chase. "They fired Tacy."

"*What?*" He stood, ready for action. "Why? When?"

Chase had his phone pressed to his ear before anyone could respond.

"Now. I was sitting in the office. I just got it. It doesn't say much. Let's march down there and ask him," Corely said.

Chase pulled the phone from his ear. "No answer. I'm going to the EDC." He headed to the door as Stefan and Corely scrambled to follow.

Chase ran right across the street between cars. He continued at that pace as he turned the corner and headed up the block to the Chamber of Commerce. He hit the front door, which he expected to be unlocked, with enough force to feel the metal door twist in its frame. The dead bolt strained to keep the door closed.

Locked. He couldn't make anything out through the glare on the windows. He looked left and right. There were cars in the square, a normal amount for a weekday morning, but no pedestrians on the sidewalks.

It didn't take much. He stepped back and sent a foot square into the door where the lock met the frame. It gave way immediately and sounded like thunder echoing back and forth between the buildings on the square.

He was several feet inside before his brain registered that there was no one there. He continued through the room towards the back door, which led to the parking lot where Tacy parked.

He turned the thumb lock and opened the rear door. There was Tacy, sitting in her truck. She was crying uncontrollably. He opened her door and gave her a hug. He pulled her to him as best he could, but her seatbelt held her back. He didn't speak.

Tacy eventually pulled away. "I can't . . . I can't believe I let that man make me cry," she said.

Chase hugged her again. Stefan and Corely appeared in the doorway, but upon seeing the pair, they turned back into the building and closed the door behind them.

Chase lowered his voice to not much more than a whisper. "Hey . . . move over and I'll drive you home."

She unbuckled herself and slid across the console to the passenger seat.

Chase drove her the short distance to her place. Tacy lived in a small duplex that Corely had helped her find. He parked and walked around to open her door, but she beat him to it. They walked inside together and Tacy excused herself to the bathroom.

Chase sat on her couch and looked over the myriad of papers on the coffee table. The living room wasn't much more than the table, couch, and her desk. There wasn't room for anything else.

The papers appeared to be for projects that had been presented to the EDC. Her handwritten notes were in the margins of many pages. There were contracts, financials, and copies of emails.

In time, Tacy reappeared from the bathroom. She looked much better, although her eyes were red. She sat next to him and put her hand on his knee. "Okay," she said.

"What happened?" Chase asked. He put his arm around her shoulders.

"He walked down there and fired me as I was opening the front door. I wasn't even to my desk."

"Who?"

"Aaron Foster. I came in the back door, and he was standing at the front waiting for me to open it."

Chase laid back, pulling Tacy into his chest. She rested her head on top of him. "He was by himself?"

"Yes. He didn't even wait for me to sit down. He said I was fired and then he left. Terminated. Effective immediately. That's what he said."

"That's it? He just left?"

"He sort of stood there for a minute and then he left without saying anything else. He didn't even lock up. I had to do it."

"You might be the first person he's ever fired."

Tacy draped her arm across Chase's chest.

"I think I can make sure I'm also the last." She sounded exceedingly tired, like she was drifting away.

The two laid there quietly. Tacy fell asleep. Chase wanted to go find Aaron Foster. The mayor too. But not as much as he wanted to lay on that couch and hold Tacy.

Chase felt his phone vibrate in his pocket. He picked up the call and spoke as quietly as he could.

It was Corely. "How's Tacy?"

"Sleeping. She's okay. What's up?"

"Aaron Foster can't fire Tacy."

"Why?"

"I'm working on that. Tell her to call me . . . oh, and Stefan fixed the door."

"What door?"

"The EDC door you worked on earlier."

"Oh. Yeah. It was in my way. Tell him thank you."

4

On a Napkin

It was easier to read the local newspaper sitting at the Butterfield than for Chase to get his own subscription. He was the first one, and maybe the only one, who seemed to read their copy anyway.

He didn't see it until he set his Americano down and settled into his seat. Sitting above the fold, on the front page, staring up at everyone, was the headline, "Who Is in Charge?" Chase knew exactly what that was about and let out an audible groan as he leaned over to pick it up.

As he was reading, the door chimed, and Stefan Beldame was soon sitting across from him.

"You read this?" Chase asked. He folded an edge of the newspaper down to make eye contact with his friend.

"I got a special preview of it from the mayor. I was summoned to his office." Stefan looked around as if to check that it was free to talk openly.

It was.

"Summoned?" Chase put the newspaper down. He had finished the article anyway.

"That's the word for it. He demanded I talk to him about calling a special meeting to rehire Tacy."

"Tomorrow night?"

"Yes. We called Aaron Foster right after we covered up your little door-kicking exercise, and he refused to tell us why they did it. Said it was a personnel matter—city business."

Chase picked up his coffee. "Tacy confirmed that isn't true. The EDC might be a city board, but it is technically a separate legal entity from the city itself."

"When I got into Turner Cam's office, he showed me the city's list of reasons. Chase, they were handwritten. After the EDC voted on the airport, Aaron Foster went back to his office and wrote out this list of complaints, signed it, dated it—that day—and put it in her file. It was basically on a napkin." Stefan knocked on the table between them as if to send the last point home.

"Is that the same list I'm looking at in the paper?"

"I trust it is. Turner told me I needed to get on the right side of this. That he had told the 'real' story to the paper and the whole town would be choosing sides. He said I needed to play ball and vote against rehiring Tacy."

"The paper says she stopped all of these big projects. They say that she cost the city dozens of jobs. All lies. These are the same projects she's been researching."

"How is she doing?"

"She's pouring herself into this. I'm just going to make sure she eats and stay out of her way."

"We've left her alone too. Corely says that's how she wants it. Who is going to tell her about this article?"

Chase stood. "I'll take this one." He shook Stefan's hand and headed out the door, the Butterfield's copy of the newspaper in his hand.

Chase figured he ought to feed her if he was going to give her bad news. Tacy wasn't a donuts and chocolate milk girl. He stopped by the gas station and got her beef jerky and possibly the worst cup of coffee in Texas. She called it "Roper's Breakfast." Maybe it would make her smile.

One silver lining of this chaos was that Chase felt like he had graduated to simply walking into Tacy's house.

He walked into the cramped front room to find Tacy sitting cross-legged in front of the coffee table. Papers were scattered everywhere, and she had a pencil in her hand scribbling notes.

She smiled when she saw him. He set her breakfast down in front of her, bent over, and delivered a kiss to her lips. His hand guided her face to his, something he got the feeling she liked. He then set the paper face down on top of the table in front of her.

"Look. You're in the paper, and it isn't great. Do you want to enjoy your breakfast first? The article can wait," Chase said as he sat on the couch.

Tacy leaned against his leg and paused for a moment. "I'm going to enjoy this delicious meal you got me, and you're going to tell me about Stefan's meeting with the mayor."

"Okay, James Bond. I didn't know I was dating a super spy." He laughed.

"Corely told me. But I want to hear your version. Entertain me while I eat."

Chase recounted the entire conversation with Stefan. He figured none of it was news to Tacy and was relieved that the article wouldn't come as a total surprise to her, except for maybe one point.

"The title of the article is 'Who Is in Charge?' and they say your rehiring would be a 'slap in the face' to everyone at the city who is doing their 'dead-level best' to help the town."

"Oh, well, Corely and I have a plan . . . of sorts."

"The Corely who Stefan said was giving you space?"

"Yes, that Corely. I'll go on the radio at noon to tell my side of the story."

Chase leaned forward. "This is where I don't think about the consequences and blindly support you?"

"Probably." She turned and kissed his knee. "Thanks."

The two spent the rest of the morning getting ready. Tacy read the newspaper and the two went over what she would say. Chase tested her computer with a link provided by the station. She would do the whole interview from there. Chase also made sure Stefan and Corely were spreading the word.

A few minutes before noon, the speakers on Tacy's laptop came to life. An assistant confirmed everything was working and then they were left to listen to the commercials that played before the show started.

After a bit, intro music played, and the host came on and delivered his boilerplate intro before introducing Tacy. "We're joined today by a special guest, Tacy Vernon. Tacy, welcome to the show. Could you tell us a little bit about your job and what brought you on the show today?"

"First, I'd like to say hello to any fellow W. R. Scurry College Westerners that may be listening. I competed there as a breakaway roper and earned a business degree before moving to Horsehead Crossing to work at your Economic Development Corporation, or what we call the EDC. I later became director and have helped a lot of small businesses get grants to help them grow and worked hard to showcase our community."

"And that came to an end this week?"

"It sure did. As you can read in the newspaper, I was fired. I'm here to set the record straight."

Music began to play.

"We're going to need to pay the bills with some commercials, but we'll be back after this break," the host said.

"You're doing great," Chase said. The two waited for a short round of ads before the show continued.

"Welcome back. We're talking to Tacy Vernon today, who is the front-page story in the newspaper. Tacy?"

"Yes, the city claims I am responsible for some major projects not coming to town. They say I cost the community dozens of jobs. The reality is very different."

"What projects?"

"First was an old building on the square donated to the city by a lifelong resident. She died without any surviving relatives. It came with the run-down parking lot that spanned every building on that side of the square."

"What was the plan for it?"

"I secured a grant to clean it all up. When I sent everything over to the city, they told me it 'was not a priority.' We can't move forward on a project without legal approval. They killed it, not me."

"So, it just sat there?"

"It was stuck in limbo. The grant deadlines passed. The city finally sold it for pennies."

"What about the other projects?"

"There was a national chain retail store looking for a potential site in town, but the city manager didn't show up to the meeting."

"Why was he a no-show?"

"He claimed he didn't know he needed to be there, but the

mayor sure did. He showed up and badgered them the whole time to go look at a very specific piece of vacant property. They finally agreed, and once they got there, he threw out an astronomical price for it. That cooled things off fast. We never heard from them again after that."

"Who owned the property?"

"The same person that bought the old building on the square on fire sale from the city."

"Are you going to tell us who that is?" Music began to play. "We need to take a break. We'll be right back."

Tacy turned to Chase. "Should I tell them?"

"We agreed not to go that far."

Music began to play again. "Welcome back. We're chatting with Tacy Vernon, who is responding to an article in today's newspaper. Tacy, this is our last segment together. Who benefited from killing these projects?"

"The only project the EDC has ever voted down is the one that got me fired. That happens to also be the only project *not* mentioned in this newspaper article. The city wanted the EDC to cosign a loan for the airport. It was a loophole to avoid borrowing the money themselves, which would have required taking the issue to the voters. The trouble for them is that the financials were terrible. The board voted it down. When you look into it more deeply, the entire airport is a playground. The pilots' lounge is a country club for the wealthy and well-connected. They come to us every year for money, but never this much. This could bankrupt us if it goes south."

"Tacy, we're out of time. Are you going to give us a name?"

"I . . . every one of those projects is tied to Baxter Whitey. Whitey bought the downtown building for nothing, and the mayor was pitching his property to the out-of-town real estate guys."

Music began to play.

"And the airport?"

The music grew louder.

"Yes. Two members of the EDC work for Whitey Family Holdings, and documents connect Baxter Whitey to the project."

"Thank you so much for your time today. That's our show. Thanks for tuning in," the host said.

5

Automagically

"We don't know if we have the votes for this," Stefan said.

He and Corely were sitting inside their small real estate office on the square. Chase and Tacy sat in guest chairs on the other side of the couple's shared desk.

"You don't think Brady Laye will vote for it?" Tacy asked.

"I tried to ask him, but he was busy. I stopped by there earlier," Stefan said.

"I guess it won't be any surprise how Baxter Whitey's people will vote," Chase said.

Whitey Family Holdings was the town's second-largest employer behind the public school system. Baxter's father had built a successful business in oil field services contributing to something called upstream oil and gas production. The family rented and serviced their impressive fleet of equipment to companies that drilled and extracted precious commodities from under this part of the Permian Basin, a collection of seven thousand oil fields which produced 40 percent of all the oil in the United States.

Baxter Whitey was also assumed to be the largest landowner

in the area. Going more than a few generations back, the family had amassed several ranches marked by a large steel *W* welded to each gated entrance. Chase couldn't travel a county road, farm road, or highway without spotting a *W* along the way.

Chase had learned all this from Stefan, his human encyclopedia.

"What worries me about Brady Laye is he got that little pep talk from the mayor the other night," Stefan said.

"This is the right thing to do. Let's just go over there and do it," Corely said.

The group exited Pecos Ranch Realty for the short walk to the Chamber of Commerce. Tacy clung to Chase's arm. There were more cars than usual on the square, all concentrated near where they were headed.

Tacy looked up to Chase and whispered, "Do you think they're here to support me?"

"Sure, baby," he lied. The radio interview was too much. Even he knew that. She had named Baxter Whitey, and there'd be a price to pay for that. He could see it on Stefan and Corely's faces as well.

Once inside, Chase was surprised to see many familiar faces. It was mainly members of Tacy's church, St. Stephen. He knew them too, but he didn't pretend like it wasn't Tacy that got him through the door of that church for the first time. As they got farther into the room, Chase felt his confidence grow. There were a lot of familiar faces in the audience.

By the time Tacy and Chase took their seats, it was past the meeting start time. The crowd quieted, and it became clear that the EDC meeting was a few board members short. Only Stefan and Corely sat around the table at the head of the room.

Stefan stood to address the crowd. "I believe you all know

why Corely and I called this special meeting. However, we can't vote on anything without a quorum. We need a third board member present. I'm afraid—"

The attention in the room shifted to the rear entrance of the building.

"Sorry I'm late," Brady Laye said. He took his seat at the table as the hushed crowd watched. "Apologies. Go ahead." He waved to Stefan with an open hand.

Chase felt a wave of relief. Three board members was a slam dunk. The crowd understood this as well. Whispers could be heard throughout the room. He squeezed Tacy's hand, and she turned to him and smiled.

Stefan took the board through the lone agenda item—the vote to rehire Tacy. It could have been 2-1, but Brady made it a unanimous vote to rehire. It was probably the shortest public meeting in town history.

Once the crowd filed out, which seemed to require everyone stopping by to thank Tacy or wish her luck, the group of friends had a chance to talk to Brady.

"I was told not to come. Turner Cam came into my store and told me not to show up. The plan was to rob you of a quorum so no vote could take place."

"How'd that work out for him?" Tacy asked.

"Not so well." Brady smiled.

"How about a celebratory beer at the Butterfield?" Stefan suggested.

"Afraid not. Honestly, I'm going to lay low for a bit. There will be backlash from this. Be safe," Brady said.

The group made the walk to the Butterfield and found that much of the meeting crowd had the same idea. Most were eating, which left the bar with only one patron.

"How ya doing, Chase? What can I get ya?" Hayden asked.

Hayden was in full hospitality mode and introduced Chase to the stranger at the bar next to him. "Do you know Blank?" he asked.

Hayden hadn't said *Blank*. He had said a name, and Chase at once forgot it. As soon as it came out of Hayden's mouth, it was lost forever. Chase had a real gift for that. He needed Tacy to remember names, but she hadn't made it to the bar yet. She was stuck at a table chatting with someone.

It turned out the man with the forgotten name ran the local radio station. Well, he was their local person, anyways—the station was owned by some conglomerate that specialized in running rural radio stations. Their format was country music, and he said that the whole thing was entirely automated. They'd hire a local freelancer to record a regular show and make other content they could plug in to give each station a local feel. Otherwise, their entire fleet of stations were run automagically from some central place.

"I live in Lubbock and cover all our stations out here, plus New Mexico. I run around and keep the wheels on all of the equipment. Normally that's an easy job, but it looks like I'm spending the night out here," he said.

"The station's been off since last night," Hayden said.

"I drove out to the tower to see why it was offline. The locks securing the building that holds all of our equipment were cut. Somebody went in there and turned it all off," the station operator said.

"No way! Did they take anything?" Chase asked. He assumed it was copper thieves or maybe high school vandals.

"No. It's all there. My guess is they just cut power to everything and that broke part of the transmitter. A new one is being overnighted, and then we cross our fingers and hope that fixes it," he said.

"They just opened the door and turned it off?" Chase asked.

"I guess so," the radio operator said. He also shared that they didn't have any cameras or any other ways of figuring out who had done it.

"So, the police are no help?" Chase asked.

"That's a corporate thing. I guess they'll handle that," the man replied.

"Isn't that wild?" Hayden asked.

Radio man was out the door before the jovial trio made it to the bar. Chase hated to throw a wet blanket on the celebration with the news. It turned out not to matter. Hayden had the story started the moment they reached the bar.

The group joked about the absurdity of it all. Everyone except Tacy. She was suddenly quiet, and it didn't look to Chase like she found any humor in the small town politics. It crushed Chase to see her mood change so fast.

Corely turned to her. "Hey, what do you plan to do now?"

"My job."

6

Pilots' Lounge

Chase's regular morning routine was only interrupted by the weekly breakfast at St. Stephen Lutheran Church. In preparation for it, he got up early to make a trip to the nearby town of Crane for breakfast burritos. Enough to feed an army.

Once back in town, he parked in line on the old, faded blacktop between where he thought the parking lines once had been painted before they were removed by time and nature. He carefully carried the bags across the lot and into the propped-open door of the church.

It was Chase's turn to contribute the main dish, and while the plain white paper sacks from Crane didn't have any distinguishing marks on them, everyone knew just what he had brought.

"We're eating good today!" exclaimed the first regular upon seeing Chase entering the church's multiuse room where the meal was served. By 7:45 the usual ten to twenty faces would be in the room. They'd chat about current events, tell stories, and then assign everyone a job to support the next breakfast.

The weekly breakfast was organized by the church's most dependable elders, but men from every corner of the community would attend. The group was a solid cross section of the town, although attendance tilted towards politicians, public servants, and retirees. While missing that day, the mayor was a regular.

Chase really enjoyed a story told that morning about how everyone around Crane had tried raising ostriches in the early 1990s. A *Time* magazine reporter had come out to interview them about it. The whole area heard about this big-time reporter's visit. This just added to the interest in ostriches and really made the whole thing sound more promising. Americans were looking for a leaner and healthier meat, and everyone thought ostrich was going to be the next big thing.

For some families, the ostrich craze was just a funny footnote, but the tone of the old rancher's story changed when he described how the initiative turned into a financial loss that some families never recovered from.

The last story of the day came from Hayden Mulvaney. He leaned in as if to tell a secret but spoke loud enough for the old-timers at the opposite end of the table to hear. "I can only tell this one because the mayor isn't with us today. Chase's girlfriend had everyone at city hall riled up yesterday."

He smiled as he continued and shot an occasional eye at the clueless Chase. "Aaron Foster, our city manager, called 9-1-1 to report that Tacy Vernon's supporters had destroyed the pilots' lounge at the airport. The windows were broken, furniture destroyed, and the ceiling tiles were ripped down. The entire inside of that place was ruined."

Chase, hearing this for the first time, was sitting in open-mouthed surprise as Hayden continued. "It took them a long time to get the footage off of the security cameras. When they did, it wasn't a mob of people upset by her radio interview. It was a jet airplane. The pilot pulled up to refuel facing the wrong direction. The jet engines were pointed at the lounge. When he went to get the plane moving again, the engines blasted the entire place. They guess the pilot probably didn't even know it happened."

The whole room remained captivated by the story as Hayden continued. "The wind from those jet engines blew open the door, broke all of the windows, and pushed every stick of furniture up against the back wall. It was like a tornado went through there."

"I would have loved to have seen the city manager's face when he first saw the video footage," one regular said. Many laughed out loud.

"The poor city manager can't add this to his file on Tacy," Hayden said.

"File?" Chase asked.

"Old Aaron Foster keeps a file on all of his enemies. He keeps tabs on everything you've ever done wrong to him."

"That's absolutely unhinged."

"I've heard it too," another regular said. Others nodded.

While the group no doubt stayed at breakfast longer than usual thanks to the entertaining story, the church elders did assign tasks for the next week, and everyone headed off in different directions to start their day.

Before Chase could get out the door, he was stopped by August Bechler. "Chase, I understand you're an FFL."

"The only one in town, actually."

"Could you stop by the place sometime? I might have some business for you."

"I'm actually free now, if that works?"

"Perfect, just give me a ten-minute head start to tidy the

place up."

August sent a location pin to Chase's phone. "A street address won't do you any good out there," August said.

Chase pointed his truck out of town towards the nearby city of McCamey until his phone told him to turn into an open ranch gate. He turned under a metal pipe that spanned the private driveway from twenty feet above, adorned with the metal letters *AB* written with a curving flare at the top and rounded angles. Serving as both a welcome and a warning, that pipe entrance separated the Running AB Ranch from the outside world.

A few lesser used roads, trails really, went off left and right into the mesquite and salt cedar trees. August owned the horizon. Chase couldn't see much beyond a few small barns and a couple larger-than-average trees in any direction. The earth just slowly fell off. However many acres he had, it was a lot.

It took a solid ten minutes to finally see a house begin to appear in the distance. As Chase drew closer, it was obvious this wasn't an average ranch house. The copper roof was the first distinguishing characteristic, followed by the sheer size of it, and then how well-kept everything was around it.

Chase felt a little out of place as he walked onto the front porch of the sprawling single-story home. The white rock and concrete porch reflected the bright sun to the point that everything appeared to glow. The entire house seemed to be made of windows, and Chase was pretty sure the door would open before he even rang the bell.

The bell itself was an antique brass knob that protruded from a round plate emblazoned with "turn here" written around the circumference. Chase hadn't seen one of these before. He grabbed the knob and turned it clockwise, which produced a unique "ring-a-ling" sound. *Ring-a-ling*. Chase wasn't sure how else to describe that bell.

And as soon as the sound rang out, the door opened, and there stood August Bechler. "Hi, Chase! How are ya?" Before waiting for an answer he said, "Come on in."

"Just fine," said Chase as he stepped into the well-lit home. Those windows really brought the light in, he thought. The ceilings in the foyer, which opened to a kitchen and entertainment area, must have been over fifteen feet high. His feet echoed on the hardwood floors as he followed August.

"Did you find the place alright?" August asked. He walked Chase around the granite-clad island in the large kitchen. "Can I get you anything?"

"No, thank you. This is a beautiful home," Chase said, paying the respects required of a guest. "How long have you been here?"

"Oh, I think about the same time as you. Maybe five years now."

"Longer than me," Chase said. He was appreciating the view of the property from the large windows in the kitchen, which looked out on a porch that matched the one on the front of the house.

"Did your business bring you out here?" August asked.

"Oh, no. I can do that from anywhere. My laptop is my office."

"Great, well can I tell you what I'm looking for?" He pointed an open hand towards Chase, who nodded for him to continue.

August took Chase through a previously closed door to the next room, which was about the size of a standard bedroom, except this one was clearly his man cave. One wall was lined with glass display cases for long guns. The opposite wall was home to three giant gun safes with three-pronged opening hardware and digital combination locks like bank vaults. The third wall was lined with a workbench, a perfectly clean workspace with a stool. A few leather chairs and a round wooden coffee table filled out the center of the room.

"Nice," Chase said, admiring the room. He walked around the cases looking at a Howa 1500, then a Savage 12 F Class, before stopping at something custom he had not seen before when he was interrupted by August, who beckoned him over to another case. That case mostly displayed Browning shotguns with ornate carvings and fine details. "I'd like to buy my first Kolar," August said.

"The only dealer for them is in San Antonio, but I can call them and figure out what they can get you. That'll be an heirloom gun. Easily $25k or more depending on the features."

"Would you like to see where I'll be shooting it?"

Chase followed August out of the kitchen and climbed into a green and yellow John Deere four-seater utility task vehicle (UTV) and headed down the driveway past the house. They turned down a trail and passed a large tank where some Corriente cattle were being watered.

The two finally arrived at a series of small metal shade structures. "We get you out of the sun as much as possible," August said. The two climbed out of the UTV.

August pointed to the tin-roofed awnings scattered about. "Next to each shade structure are stands. The throwers are in those little tin huts down there," he explained.

August had built his own private course for sporting clays, a sport sometimes called "golf with a shotgun." August had an elaborate setup of machines that would throw a clay disc to mimic the travel of a duck, dove, or even bounce along the ground like a rabbit. Each shooter would take their turn trying to break the clay with the spray of a shotgun. Competitors would travel around to different "holes," or stations where the configuration was slightly different. The number of clays successfully broken was the score.

The two headed back in the UTV as Chase answered questions about his business. He held a Federal Firearms License (FFL) with the ATF, which allowed him to buy and sell guns. He also did a little gunsmithing, where he'd make repairs or customize a gun, but mostly on guns he was flipping to other dealers.

"And this makes good money?" August asked.

"Not really. The big money is in importing ammunition and a little military surplus from overseas. That's ITAR stuff with the secretary of state—International Traffic in Arms Regulations. There's bonded warehouses and a whole mess of paperwork," Chase said.

And with that August extended a future invitation back out to his place. "I want to hear more about this, as well as what your girlfriend has gotten herself into over at the city. Come out when my shooting buddies are around. I'll send you an invite. Bring your shotgun."

7

Sporting Clays

It had been a very quiet week. Silent really. Tacy mentioned that it worried her. She was on the upcoming city council agenda for two back-to-back items. She'd provide her regular update, which she said felt far from regular, as well as get her annual budget approved.

She was also still looking into city finances and projects. Chase tried his best to help, but he was mostly reduced to just brief check-ins. He was the "world's most handsome food delivery guy," Tacy had joked.

Chase started his day at the Butterfield, checked on Tacy, and then pointed his truck towards McCamey. He turned under the Running AB pipe entrance and led a cloud of dust right up to August Bechler's house. August and two other guys were standing on the porch as he pulled up.

August looked like a rancher, but the other two wore synthetic fishing shirts and cargo pants made of similar fabric. Chase joked to himself that they looked like gray men, or sheepdogs. Those were gun culture terms for plainclothes security that tried so hard to blend in they ended up sticking out.

That fit these two. Each had the not-so-subtle bulge of a concealed handgun on his waist, forward of the hip, in a position known as appendix carry. Chase also knew the brands of their untucked shirts—one a Huk and the other a Burlebo. Both were expensive and sold in one of the struggling boutiques in town. These men were athletic, armed, and wearing expensive shirts.

August was the first to speak. "Hey, Chase! Meet Max and Diego." He pointed with an open hand to each as he said their name.

Max, closest to Chase and the first to extend his hand, looked like a runner. "Chase, I'm Max. Nice to meet you."

Chase could only nod in response because the next hand was already extended to him. "I'm Diego. Good to see you." The most noticeable thing about him was that his ears were lumpy and misshapen. Chase recognized it from his years of high school wrestling.

You don't mess with a guy with a cauliflower ear, he reminded himself silently before exchanging greetings. The three were friendly, but their body language as he walked up gave Chase the impression that he had interrupted a conversation. "It looked like you guys were in the middle of it, I'll unpack my gun," he said.

"We're just talking about Spud Locker. It's a conference we go to every year," Diego said.

"Oh, you guys all work together?" asked Chase. He noticed that everyone was wearing hats with matching logos.

"Well, yes, but this is for a nonprofit. We basically play golf, run a 5k, and have a black-tie banquet during three days of drinking," said Max. The group laughed.

Diego must have sensed that some further clarification was

needed. "Yeah, man, we flew together in the Navy. Everyone at the event is an aviator. It's a big party. The three of us were sent to Norfolk after the 9/11 attacks. We flew Hummers up and down the East Coast."

"The truck?" Chase asked, thinking flying Hummers was slang for driving a Humvee.

"No, the giant frisbee-looking turboprop. Airborne Early Warning. The eye in the sky," Max said. "Airplanes with a bunch of radar equipment."

"They can see everything. We basically glow in the dark after a career flying a giant X-ray machine," Diego said.

"But, yes, we also still work together. We work government contracts," August said.

"Like guns for hire?" Chase asked, only halfway joking.

"Much less exciting," August said with a laugh. "We help the big federal contractors with some really niche computer systems. The work isn't steady, but it pays well when it comes. We have a few retired Air Force guys that don't mind the ups and downs. Otherwise, we keep an eye out for contracts for anything we think a big player would overlook. Last year, we had guys drive all over Texas doing an inventory of office furniture for some bean counters in a state agency."

The four moved inside as the conversation turned to their time flying in the Navy, their lives since, and the company they ran together. They explained that some of the contracts granted to the likes of Lockheed, Raytheon, Northrop, General Dynamics, and SAIC had small parts that would fall through the cracks to them. "We don't mind paperwork," said Diego. That got him a sly smile from August.

"Okay, three Navy buddies have a bunch of Air Force guys doing government contracts, and you shoot guns together in your free time," Chase said.

"Bingo!" Diego confirmed. "How'd you get in the gun business?"

"A few years ago, I reconnected with a high school buddy that built AR-15s. Cheap ones. Really, he just assembled them, and he could sell them as fast as he put them together. My parents were sick, and I was home taking care of them. I figured if he could do it, I could do it. It was just to make some extra money," Chase said.

Assembling guns didn't turn out to be as lucrative as his buddy had made it sound. However, it had paid well enough for him to finance an opportunity to import a pallet of cheap ammunition made of steel instead of brass. "The COVID outbreak had people stockpiling whatever they could get their hands on," Chase said.

"Sounds like you don't mind a little paperwork yourself!" Max joked.

"Nope," Chase said.

"Let's go shoot some clays. While we're out there, Chase can tell you guys about his time in France," August said.

"France? How'd you hear about that?" Chase asked.

"A little bird told me," August said. "But really, I poked around before I had you order that Kolar."

Chase was floored. Maybe he was even a little impressed. Mad? No. A bit puzzled, though. "Dang, man. What blood type am I?"

"No worries, buddy. August would be a terrible spy. He just asked us to make sure you weren't a weirdo," Diego said.

He looked over at Max who chimed in. "But data isn't a good story. I'm betting you have a good story."

"I spent six years with MarinMédecins. It's a hospital ship

based in France. Most of the time we anchored around Africa. I joined when I was eighteen, like a week after high school graduation," Chase said.

"You just left home and got a job on a floating hospital in a foreign country? Who does that?!" Max asked.

"I told my parents I was doing a gap year in Europe!" Chase laughed at the absurdity of the lie he'd fed his parents. "I wasn't a wild kid, but I didn't fit in and sure didn't like school. I did just enough to get by and stay on the wrestling team." The group piled into the UTV and headed away from the house. Chase had to speak over the noisy utility vehicle.

"I'd later tell my mom it was all her fault. Jokingly. We had to take a foreign language, and my mom insisted I take French. That's the only class I ever paid attention in. My teacher was pretty. She could keep a young man's attention, if you know what I mean."

The group laughed.

The UTV continued noisily down the trail.

"Anyway, I read about the French Foreign Legion, then about this ship that sailed around the world supplying medical services in places that wouldn't otherwise have them."

"You just wanted to be Jean-Claude Van Damme!" Max joked in reference to the 1998 movie *Legionnaire.*

"I was a baby when that came out!" was Chase's retort.

"Yeah, in diapers!" returned Max.

Chase went on to tell them he spent six years mostly in Africa supporting UN peacekeeping missions. The guys got a kick out of his job as a purser, which they all admitted was somehow even more boring than it sounded. He managed customs documents for any country the ship visited, the inventory of supplies, and lots of paperwork.

"Then my parents got sick, and I went home to take care of them."

By this time the group had stopped the UTV at the first stand and begun setting up for sporting clays. Chase shot last and did so with a semiautomatic Remington that was unimpressive other than easily being seventy years old.

Chase left the first stand tied with August and Max. Diego trailed behind. Between turns, Chase told the story of his parents passing away within a year of each other. He hinted it was too close together for him to properly process, but he didn't provide any details.

"It was like winning some terrible lottery. Cancer sucks." They all agreed.

At one point, August pulled him aside. "This is usually a business weekend. We spend these shoots reviewing company financials and deciding which contracts to pursue. We'll have a whole team out here tonight, so if we shoo you out of here in a few hours, don't feel bad about it."

"Not a problem," Chase said.

"We got a good thing going. We plan our revenue targets for the quarter, and once they're met, we prioritize our spare time. Work to live, not live to work."

At the "turn," the halfway point in the match, it was August and Chase at the top. Max had struggled with the unpredictable bounces of a station that rolled the clays across the ground. "The rabbit got me."

Chase continued to tell the group about how moving had been a fresh start, one he had prepared for with his parents. "They worked their whole lives waiting for retirement only to never see it. They didn't want that for me."

Chase wasn't sure if August was taking it easy on him or not, but station after station they remained within striking distance of each other.

At the last station, it was Chase's match for the taking. The high arching clays were a tough shot. That was when August showed the value of home field advantage. Max, Diego, and Chase struggled to break half of the clays. August broke all of his and won the day.

"Congrats, August! Nice shooting." Chase patted him on the back. Max and Diego murmured something about the matches always going that way.

"We have just enough time to get ready for dinner. Nice shooting," August said.

On the drive back to the house, the group asked Chase to continue his story about the grand plan he'd hatched with his parents. He told them how he took a modest inheritance and looked for a piece of rental property in a new town. A fresh start.

"That's how I ended up owning the building where the flower shop is, next to the Butterfield. Now I'm landlord and handyman."

"And you raise chickens and sell guns?" Max asked.

"Yup. Add it all up, and I might make a living."

"And shoot well enough to give August a run for his money!"

"How is it that a purser can shoot so well?" Diego asked.

Chase laughed, but didn't offer an answer.

8

Certificate of Deposit

Chase walked right into Tacy's with breakfast in hand. She briefly poked her head out of her bathroom. "Roper's Special?"

Chase laughed. "No, brisket omelet. From the new BBQ place."

She yelled back from the bathroom, "They serve breakfast?"

"Ma'am, somebody made this, and I assure you it wasn't me."

"Funny. Did you see the final city council agenda?"

"No, can't say I have."

She poked her head back into the hallway. "Now there's three EDC items up for discussion. The new one mentions the board but doesn't provide any detail."

"You're going to have to eat this in the truck." He held up the Styrofoam container.

"Don't want to be late. They might fire me!" she said with a smile.

Chase enjoyed seeing her in a good mood. He dropped her off in the decaying parking lot behind the EDC and left with an assignment. He promised her he'd try to figure out what the city council planned to do in the meeting that night. His first stop was Stefan's office across the street.

Chase parked in front and walked through the door expecting to see Stefan, who kept a pretty consistent daily routine. Instead, he found both Stefan and Corely.

"Two for one deal. What's up?" Chase asked.

"We got an early morning wake-up call from Turner Cam," Stefan said.

"Oh." The smile left Chase's face. "What happened?" He took a seat across from the couple's desk.

"So much for this being an easy volunteer position where we just rubber-stamp grants for mom-and-pop businesses," Corely said.

Stefan added his thoughts. "He called us and told us to resign or the city council would kick us off the board. They can do it too. They appointed us, and they can kick us off. They did the same thing to Brady Laye."

"Brady was threatened too?" Chase asked.

"Yes, and he resigned," Stefan replied.

"And you two?" Chase feared he knew the answer.

"I told Turner this was bull, and he didn't even disagree with me. I saw the agenda too. They were ready to kick us off. I don't need this," Stefan said.

"We're relieved to be off," Corely said.

Chase felt his heart sink.

"What about Tacy?" he asked.

Stefan started to speak. "I—"

Chase stood. "What about Tacy?" He spoke more forcibly.

"The city council has the votes and the authority to get rid of us," Corely said.

"How is she supposed to react to this?" Chase asked.

"She'll understand. She has to. We didn't have a choice," Corely said.

Stefan's eyes were glued to the floor.

"I bet she won't," Chase said. He stormed out of their office and left his truck parked where it was. The two hurried after him, on his hip as he walked to the EDC and through the unlocked front door.

As he entered the building, he had to duck to miss a paper-weight flying at his head.

"Get out of my office!" Tacy yelled.

Chase held up his hands while looking for the next projectile. "What did I do?"

She picked up a stapler. "The mayor called. They resigned from the board and didn't even tell me!" She hurled the stapler at him. Chase heard it whiz by.

"I didn't do anything!"

Tacy picked up a metal water bottle. "Get out! All of you!"

"Hold on!" He held his hands up ready to defend himself. Corely and Stefan were already out the door.

Tacy threw the bottle. It practically exploded when it hit the floor. Water was everywhere.

"Get out!" she screamed.

"Okay, okay," Chase said. He backed out of the door.

He walked back to his truck, leaving the Beldames standing in silence on the sidewalk. They didn't speak or attempt to follow him. He started his truck and drove home.

He assumed Tacy would call at some point. Surely, she would know that Chase wasn't involved. How could he be?

He just sat. Doing nothing. Eventually, he had lost the whole day and had to force himself to get up. He couldn't watch the city council meeting online. He had to be there.

A city council meeting was a far bigger event than any EDC meeting, and this one was even bigger than most. The rumor mill, likely aided by the radio interview as well as the newspaper article, had generated sufficient interest in the meeting as to make it standing room only. No doubt a large group was also watching the events unfold on Facebook, where the meeting was streamed live.

When the mayor called the first person up to the podium for public comments, it was an older rancher that took his time getting up there. Chase heard his boots shuffle across the floor, although all he could see from his seat was the man's back, hunched from age, slowly moving towards the microphone.

The man spoke as slowly as he walked. "I got my water bill." He pulled a piece of paper from the pocket of his shirt. "You can barely drink what comes out of the tap, but it still cost me $125."

Not a single city council member bothered to look up at the man as he spoke.

He continued, "I had to dodge potholes on the way through town. Some of them were big enough to lose a car in."

Chase guessed that the disinterest of the assembled city leaders was because this was a message they heard at every meeting.

"Anyway, I think we ought to finally get this fixed. We've had these problems my whole life, and all everyone in charge has said is that it's too big of a problem. Well, maybe we need to start thinking of some big solutions." He stood there silently for a moment. Chase thought that maybe he was waiting for an answer. Perhaps there'd be some acknowledgment. Instead, the city leaders kept their heads down, looking at agendas or other papers in front of them.

The old rancher shuffled away from the podium at the same speed he arrived. It took the mayor a moment to recognize that he was finished and that it was time for the next speaker.

The second person to comment had no problem getting the attention of everyone in the room.

"When the devil comes to breakfast, you have to make sure you aren't on the menu," he said. The middle-aged man spoke from under a felt cowboy hat. "Right now, it feels like this town is on the menu. Who do you all work for?"

He paused, but none of the leaders made an effort to respond.

The man went on to deliver comments that were almost a verbatim retelling of Tacy's radio interview. When his three minutes were up, the mayor rapped his gavel on the table, which echoed through the room. The noise was louder than Chase expected, and it surprised him. The loud noise was enough to bring the comments to an end. The man quietly returned to his seat.

The final speaker was visibly nervous as she approached the podium, unlike the slow and deliberate delivery of the first two. But she seemed to shake it off. With a determined tilt of her head, she launched into an impassioned speech.

"You treat the EDC like a personal piggy bank! Is this okay?"

"You pushed a project that loses money! Is this okay?"

"You have to pass it to know what's in it! Is this okay?"

"If you get in the way, you're fired! Is this okay?"

She went on and on, repeating every point made by the previous speaker. When her three minutes were up, the mayor banged his gavel.

She didn't stop. She kept on.

"Ma'am, your time is up!" the mayor yelled.

She persisted with her questions until finally the mayor

waved at the deputy leaning against the wall.

"Deputy, please escort that woman from this meeting!" he shouted over her.

She stopped speaking as the deputy approached. Chase thought that he appeared to be a reluctant participant; he had an exchange with the woman that no one else could hear. She left the podium and walked out of the building while the deputy returned to his post.

"I'm the mayor, and I'm going to have decorum in these meetings!" he said. He pushed his chair back from the table. He threw his gavel, and it loudly struck the wooden table in front of him, knocking his nameplate askew and spreading his papers around irregularly. "We're adjourned for five minutes." He then left the room, his face glowing red.

No one in the crowd stirred. This must have been their first Turner Cam temper tantrum.

After the break, the city council returned to a full room, and routine business followed. Like probably every meeting of politicians in the world, it was boring.

When they reached her items on the agenda, Tacy took the podium. Chase had been looking for her and didn't see where she had come from.

Tacy had to stand there while the city council appointed new members to the EDC. They chose three council members to simultaneously sit on the EDC board. Finally, an emotionless Tacy was able to brief them on her agenda items.

Tacy went through what appeared to be a regular rundown of active projects. She detailed a grant they were pursuing from the state for money to improve the sidewalks around downtown businesses as well as the status of all the grants the EDC had awarded to local businesses in the last few months.

The tone for the rest of the meeting shifted when she began to talk about her budget. A council member, one who had just been named to the EDC board, began asking her about interest rates being paid on the EDC's money being held at a local bank.

He held a newspaper high in his hand, opened to a bank advertisement for a CD, or a certificate of deposit, which he said paid 5 percent interest. For the next twenty-five very long minutes, Tacy walked the council member through her recent financial review of accounts at the bank and how taxpayer money couldn't be put into regular accounts like the one in the ad.

Each second of the exchange etched deeper lines of frustration in the face of the council member. He remained convinced that she wasn't properly managing EDC money.

The audience was shifting in their seats from the growing discomfort. It appeared to Chase that the council member was caught in a web of financial ignorance of his own making. As the conversation continued, the newspaper in his hand sank lower and lower.

Finally, his veneer of authority had cracked enough for a fellow council member to take over questioning. The second council member, who also had just been named to the EDC board, was like a cat waiting for his prey. "Who pays the salary of the EDC director?"

"When the voters created the EDC, they set aside a portion of sales tax revenue, and those funds pay for all of our initiatives, including my salary," Tacy said. Her delivery was deadpan. Chase was surprised she didn't seem upset by any of this.

"Does it say EDC on your pay stub?" he asked. He knew he had her.

"No, the check is cut by the city," she replied.

"Because you are an employee of the city," he said. A smile escaped his lips. It looked to Chase that he even glanced over to the mayor and the city manager.

"We transfer EDC funds to the city for my pay and benefits. This is EDC money," she said. The prey had escaped.

The two went back and forth belaboring the same points; Tacy's expressionless replies seemed to spur him on. She showed no emotion as a third council member joined the fray. He was, unsurprisingly, the final member added to the EDC that night.

"You were fired by this body and then rehired by the EDC since you last appeared here?" he asked.

"On that point, no one at the city has returned a call or email of mine since I was rehired. I know that at least one very important meeting occurred this week without me. Plus there's some very serious account—"

Aaron Foster interrupted her. "This wasn't a legal hire. The EDC doesn't have a director. This isn't even a valid update."

"I think we've had enough," the mayor said. He was a normal color as he continued, "Do I have a motion?"

"I'm still giving my report! You can't sweep these problems under the rug!" Tacy's raised voice was once again cut off, this time by the mayor.

"You're done! Do I have a motion?" the mayor asked.

"I move that we table the EDC budget," said the council member who had been questioning Tacy about her position.

"Seconded," said the one that had received an unwanted financial lesson.

"Any discussion?" Turner Cam asked.

The only one to speak was one of the council members who had sat quietly all night. "I don't like where this conversation

53

went tonight. We can't operate an EDC without a budget. How do they pay for anything without an approved budget? How do they pay their director?"

No one responded. Turner looked over the group, allowing time for anyone else to chime in. No one else spoke. "All in favor?" he asked.

Three hands went up in support—the three new EDC board members.

"All opposed?" he asked.

Hands went up from the remaining two council members.

"The motion passes three to two," Turner Cam said.

Tacy, still at the podium, spoke again, "I resign from my position." With that, she promptly turned and walked to a door leading to a part of the building Chase wasn't familiar with. That must have been how she entered the room without him noticing.

Before she reached the door, she turned towards the town's leaders and yelled, "This isn't the end of this!"

As she exited the room, members of the audience began to stand. They filed out the door to the street outside. The first to get up were quickly followed by others. Both council members that voted no rose from their seats and joined the growing crowd outside.

They were all walking out on an active city council meeting. Turner Cam stood and loudly rapped his gavel on the desk. As he did, he spoke over the growing chatter of the departing crowd, "This meeting is adjourned!" He disappeared quickly, followed by Aaron Foster, out the same door Tacy had just used.

9

Locked Gates

Chase followed everyone outside, but there was no sign of Tacy. Wherever she went, she got there without being stopped by anyone. He looked up the street towards her office—her old office—as his phone rang.

"Yeah?" He answered the phone just to avoid interacting with anyone. He wasn't in the mood to chat.

It was Stefan. "We watched the meeting. What happened?"

"I don't know, man. They stacked the board, gave Tacy a hard time, and then basically told her they weren't going to pay her anymore." Chase began walking towards Tacy's office. "Anyway, I'm busy."

"Is Tacy with you? We just left her a message."

"No, I'm looking for her now." He was finally clear of the crowd, which was still assembled. All he heard as he left was loud gossip. Maybe it was all just entertainment for them. A show.

"We're sorry. We aren't going to make excuses. We just ask for forgiveness."

"I'm going to need a minute on that one."

Maybe all the town wanted to see was the conflict. Maybe they didn't really care.

"Could you meet us at the Butterfield?"

"I have to run, man." Chase ended the call.

Chase looked into the window of the Chamber of Commerce. It was dark. He then walked the entire block to get to the backside of the building where Tacy parked.

He had just missed her. As he turned the corner, he saw her truck driving off.

He began to jog halfheartedly after her, but he knew he couldn't catch up. "Hey!" Chase yelled despite knowing Tacy couldn't hear him from that distance.

Her truck was rapidly out of sight.

Chase stood there, hands on hips, as a city truck pulled out on the same street and headed off in the same direction. Some city employees were in a hurry to get out of there. Chase couldn't blame them.

He picked up his phone and tried to call her. He knew she wouldn't answer. Maybe in a day or two, but no way she'd be ready to talk yet. Sure enough, it went to voicemail. He didn't leave a message. He wasn't sure what to say.

Chase stood shell-shocked. His mind drifted. He remembered how Stefan once told him the author Zane Grey described this part of Texas: *desolate, gray, and lonely.*

Fitting.

Chase stood there in the dark as a few other cars made it out of city hall, destined for wherever. The streets were quickly quiet again.

Chase started walking towards Tacy's. That did not take him in the direction her truck had gone, but perhaps she'd be home by the time he got there. Where else would she be?

He had thought about going to the Butterfield, as if every-thing was okay, but then thought better of it.

The walk did Chase some good. He mostly focused on navigating the broken sidewalks in the dark. Despite being in the center of town, most of the lots were vacant. The only activity on the street was a cat that ran by with what looked like a lizard in its mouth.

There were no street lights in this part of town. Most of the houses had a sliver of light pouring out onto the street from a front window or a small porch light. Tacy's place, a duplex, was dimly lit from a cheap little light that hung over her door. Chase turned the knob and pushed, but the door didn't budge. It was locked.

He leaned over to the large picture window then looked into her tiny living room. Nothing. No lights. He walked off the porch and around the driveway to the carport on the back side of the place. No truck.

Chase turned on his heels and pointed his toes to the Butter-field. The walk back seemed to take longer. He almost tripped on a few uneven pieces of concrete.

He got all the way to the Butterfield, his hand resting on the door, before he changed his mind. He turned and walked up the block. He went past the faded fiftieth anniversary sign that hung in the window of the flower shop. At the end of the block, he turned and went to the back of the building.

The buildings on that side of the square were identical. The two-story squares of brick were all high-ceilinged spaces with no actual second floor. His flower shop was the exception.

A set of back stairs led up to Chase's apartment. Instead of climbing them, he walked across the alley to the metal building that housed his truck and tools. It was his own private space tucked between similar buildings.

The process of parking in the metal workshop had gotten old. Chase opened the heavy roll-up door, backed his truck out, and then had to get out to roll the door back down.

His truck sat in the alley while his headlights illuminated the other jewel of his property. The large fenced-in dirt lot had come with his building and metal shop. It was a chicken run, a safe area for chickens to roam without the worry of predators. Within that run was a coop that had fallen into disrepair. Stefan had given him the idea of fixing it up and restarting an earlier owner's egg business. That's exactly what he had done. Seeing the coop reminded him of the work that was waiting for him there in the morning. Every morning.

Chase drove his truck out of town in the direction Tacy had gone. Once past the few homesteads and small businesses, there wasn't anything but oil field roads until he reached the town of Crane.

Chase kept his head on a swivel as he headed south through town and then back to McCamey.

There were several more oil field roads. Chase and Tacy knew a couple of them, but not well enough to navigate in the dark. Hidden in the desert were a pair of lakes they'd visit, Juan Cordona Lake and Soda Lake. Neither one would have more than a foot of water. Tacy knew all about their history. It had been a hundred years since commercial traders had stopped pulling salt out of them, a once-booming industry that had started with the Apache.

He was confident he could not navigate the maze of oil field roads to find either lake in the dark. Tacy probably couldn't either. Even if he tried, he'd meet a locked gate this time of night. The only way to access those lakes was during the daytime. Even then, a departing oil field crew could lock the gate without warning. Tacy thought that was most of the fun.

After some time, Chase pulled off the highway to think. He had a perfect view of both King Mountain and Castle Mountain. The bright moonlight lit them up perfectly. An opening, known as Castle Gap, sat between the two and resembled a castle with a hole in its wall. Early travelers would use the landmark to navigate to the Pecos River, one of the few sources of drinking water in the region. Tacy could recount all of this history.

She probably would have liked the hike on such a clear night. She liked to be alone when she was mad anyway. However, all of Castle Gap was private property, and there's no way she could navigate the roads and locked gates in the dark.

She'll blow off steam and call me tomorrow, Chase thought to himself. Just to be sure, he continued on to McCamey before turning back home. He never saw her truck.

10

Kitchen Door

Chase sat next to Corely and Stefan at the Butterfield's bar as a few other locals ate at the four-top tables. The three sat there like everything was okay. Like Tacy hadn't ignored all of them for twenty-four hours. Like they had even seen Tacy much less heard from her.

Hayden was filling them in on the latest gossip. It came from that radio station guy. "The AM station is down for good. Whoever broke into the tower also cut the cable going to the red safety lights that mark the tower for airplanes."

The three friends had not actually spoken yet. Hayden had saved them from exchanging awkward greetings with his story.

"When the tower went down, someone called the FAA, and the station got in trouble for not having safety lights to warn passing airplanes."

"Someone turned the tower lights off and then called the feds to file a complaint? Sounds a little fishy," Corely said.

"It's worse than that. Someone also called the FCC. They said that the tower was unsafe, which means it has to be inspected," Hayden said.

"I bet that's expensive. I watched a show about the guys that climb those towers. Deadliest job in America. They're called tower dogs," Stefan said. He was a fount of random knowledge.

"That's not even the crazy part. While all this was happening, the person that owns the land under the tower offered to decommission it for free. Save the radio station the cost and trouble. Guess who that is," Hayden said.

"Who?"

"Baxter Whitey."

"Right after Tacy goes on the radio, the tower gets shut down. Then along comes Baxter Whitey to put the final nail in the coffin at just the right time?" Corely scoffed.

"I don't know, but the radio guy said corporate jumped at his offer," Hayden replied.

Chase still hadn't touched his beer.

Corely seemed happy to put words to what he was thinking. "The mayor, city manager, and Baxter are pushing an airport project so hard that they worked together to fire Tacy, appoint a new EDC board, and then shut down the radio station for giving the other side airtime?"

"I don't know," Chase said, finally speaking.

"This only sounds crazy to someone who isn't from here," Corely said. "I'm not sure they've ever been openly opposed before."

"For sure," Hayden agreed.

"No one's ego is that fragile," Chase said.

"Well, there's the principle of Occam's Razor. The simplest explanation is usually the best one. They're just ticked someone told them no," Stefan said.

"I think there's more to it. Tacy found something. Something bigger than the airport just being a questionable investment.

I'm not sure what is because I don't think she's sure yet either," Chase said.

"I think Tacy probably had enough of this place, and I can't blame her for it. I don't think she's barhopping in New Orleans or backpacking Europe, but she's probably with rodeo friends blowing off steam," Corely said.

"What friends?" Chase asked. "Her friends are all right here."

"Her old roommate from college, for one," Corely replied.

"Or maybe she's living on a ship in Africa," Stefan said, eyeing Chase.

"What in the world, man? Where'd you hear that?"

"Word in town is you lived on a boat. Like as a nurse or something."

"And what else?" asked Chase.

"What do you mean? Working as a floating nurse turning down beds for sick kids in Africa isn't something you'd mention to your friends?" Stefan asked.

August would make a terrible spy. He had obviously told them about Chase's time with MarinMédecins. The Beldames thought it was funny their friend had an "exotic" past, as they called it. They wanted to hear all about it, but Chase made the job sound boring enough that the story was short.

He wasn't going to explain what it meant to be what they called a *bon camarade*—a good fellow. He wouldn't explain that any more than he'd explain what it was like losing his parents or how he had wanted them to fight to stay on the EDC board or how it felt having August tell them about his past.

Chase finally took a sip of his beer, and the prolonged silence thankfully moved the conversation back to Tacy.

"We found her a job," Stefan said.

Corely added, "At the Chamber of Commerce. I think they'd hire her. They have budget for a position. They just need to get off their backsides. That's what we left her a message about."

Stefan looked to Chase. "Do you really think something is wrong?"

"I'm not sure Tacy is okay," Chase said. "These people are nuts, and I'm going to do something about it. She was going to say something. I don't know what, but I'm going to figure it out. I'm not going to sit here and pretend everything is okay." He stood from the bar.

"I drove by her place twice today. She isn't there. I think we just have to give her time," Corely said.

"If she doesn't show up soon, we can talk to the sheriff. That's the right move," Stefan said.

"If you're worried, you can talk to the sheriff," Chase said. "I'm going to actually do something about this." He walked out of the Butterfield without another word.

* * *

He hoped to see her car in the carport, but it wasn't there. Chase parked in her spot and walked to the wooden gate in her fence. Thankfully, it was unlocked and opened silently. His heart was racing even though he had been there dozens of times.

This was different.

Chase hoped to find Tacy's kitchen door unlocked. Otherwise, he'd need it to have a missing or poorly fitting stop, a thin strip of material that covers the small gap between the doorjamb and strike plate. He could sneak his pocketknife into the gap to force open the latch bolt.

As Chase approached the door, it was obvious that it was

new and well-constructed. He tried it anyway only to find it locked. He looked around and could see into the neighbors' yards, which meant if they were looking in that direction, they could see him too. He was no different than a common prowler. A midnight burglar. Working on this door for any time would just add risk to a situation that already felt like it was getting out of hand. He didn't know her neighbors and they didn't know him. They would clearly see he wasn't the cute young cowgirl that lived there.

Only two windows faced the backyard, and Chase tried them both. Locked and new, which meant he couldn't get through them without the noise of breaking glass. He decided to go back over to the gate where he would be out of sight and could catch his breath. He was getting into that house. Somehow.

Back through the gate, he circled the driveway. There was one small window, clearly visible from the street, but different from the rest with its frosted glass. Her bathroom. It looked like it wasn't fully shut. Sure enough, the window moved up as he put his hand against the glass.

Because the window was smaller and higher off the ground than the rest, it took some effort for Chase to lift himself up and through it. Once in, he quickly closed the window behind him without bothering to check if anyone had seen him. His heart was beating in his ears.

The bathroom was small and clean. He opened a drawer and saw it was full of toiletries. While he knew he was alone, he still stepped quietly across the bathroom and into the hallway. He moved slowly because the only light was what came through the windows. Once in the hallway, he was in complete darkness and had to turn on the screen of his smartphone to see.

The hallway connected the bedroom to the living room. He

went to the bedroom first, which was as perfectly kept as the bathroom. The bed was made. Her room wasn't even big enough for a chair. There was just a nightstand, a chest of drawers, and a small closet. Each of these was full of clothes— nothing that caught his attention.

Chase went back out to the front room. He always thought it was funny that her living room was so untidy while the rest of her little duplex was spotless and organized. The cramped room always left a comically small amount of space to navigate around.

On Tacy's desk was the power adapter for her laptop, which wasn't there. She had stacks of papers, some in folders, that he began to sort through by the light of his phone. There were random bills, a couple of old tax returns, and other stacks that didn't seem to be of importance. The folders were labeled insurance, car stuff, and utilities. Chase then moved to her coffee table where Tacy had her work papers from the EDC.

She had gone over all of this with him before. There were contracts, budget spreadsheets, and some handwritten notes. Her notes always took a second to read through. Tacy wrote in cursive, which he thought was funny. The light from his phone made it a frustrating read, but these were all airport financials. Her notes showed multiple errors across several years of reports. They didn't make perfect sense, but mostly because there was so much information.

She had also written on an airport contract that Chase had not seen before. She must have just gotten it. These documents were the only thing even close to being interesting. He thought about taking all of her documents to her closet to photograph them. No one would see the camera flash from there. Instead, he just took them. All of them. A whole armful.

He made one more trip around the apartment. The kitchen looked normal. Her bedroom looked normal. No clothes seemed to be missing. Her bathroom, also normal. *No one goes on a trip without their toothbrush*, Chase thought.

With his arms full of documents, Chase decided to walk right out the back door. He pressed the little button lock on the knob as he pulled the door closed behind him. He tried his best to control his pace back to his truck, but it felt like he was practically speedwalking. He could picture a neighbor confronting him, but he made it to the truck without encountering anyone.

11

White Knight

After a fitful night's sleep, Chase bolted out of bed with an idea. He dialed his phone ignoring the time. It only rang once.

"Chase?" August Bechler asked.

"Hey, I've got a problem. Can I bring you something?"

"You bet."

"I'm headed your way."

As Chase drove to Running AB Ranch, he was mentally going over the documents he got from Tacy's. It was a sea of information. He wasn't sure how he'd explain it all.

The smell of fresh coffee hit Chase in the face when he stepped into August's front room. He dropped his load of documents on the living room table and started to explain as much as he could.

"Hold on," August said. "The guys are in the bunkhouse and will be coming up for breakfast. How about you run this past all three of us?"

August poured Chase a cup of coffee and busied himself in the kitchen. Within thirty minutes both Max and Diego had joined them and were eating bacon and eggs as Chase unloaded everything he had.

At the end of each year, a city employee would measure how much fuel was left in the gas tanks at the airport. This aviation fuel was bought by the city, stored in tanks at the airport, and resold for a profit. The value of any fuel still in the tanks at the end of the year should be moved to the financial reports for the next year. However, the city was erasing the costs at the end of the year instead of moving them. This made the airport look more profitable than it was.

Tacy had copies of city documents that detailed how much fuel was recorded by city workers. She also had the monthly financials that proved the leftover fuel at the end of one year never showed up on the report for the next year. Thousands of dollars of costs simply vanished.

She had also discovered that the financials for previous years were being changed. If someone wanted to know what it cost to run the airport in the past year, they could get as many as four different answers depending on which city report they looked at. What she didn't have were the matching bank records that would show if the money was being moved or maybe even stolen.

Chase might have sounded like a madman sitting in front of August, Max, and Diego. He was dumping information into the room just as he'd dumped the documents on the table. He wasn't even waiting to see if they were following along as he raced from document to document.

Finally, Chase began to explain the last thing he thought Tacy had uncovered. She had assembled a list of all the money the EDC had sent to the airport over the years. It wasn't as much as Chase had expected, but it was a steady flow. Tacy thought the airport might be falsifying their profitability, making up for the shortcoming with EDC money, and then editing their financials to hide it all.

"Stefan said that it isn't unusual for an EDC to regularly invest in a local airport," said August. "Someone might say these are unrelated errors or poor management." He took a sip of coffee.

"How do you know Stefan, again?" asked Chase.

"He sold me this place."

"Oh." Chase picked up his cup. "I'm not sure I knew that."

"He's a good guy. We should bring him in on this. I know you were disappointed with his decision to resign from the board without a fight."

"No, I get it. I think it was more how Tacy reacted to it."

"Let's pull him in to create a battle plan."

"I don't have time. I was hoping you'd run with these financials while I find Tacy. Figure out if, or how, this is all connected. Something's wrong."

"Stefan's connections will be valuable. This is a closed community. We could live our whole lives here and not have the access he does. I'll start my guys on this if you at least give him a chance."

"Fine. Okay. I need to call him anyway, but I'm headed straight out to Snyder to look for Tacy. That's where she went to school and there's a big rodeo out there this weekend."

"I'll send one of these guys with you," August said.

* * *

Max joked that he drew the short straw as he accompanied Chase to W. R. Scurry College in Snyder, Texas. He even offered to drive, which was okay with Chase, as three hours on the road in a Ford Explorer was better than his old truck.

"I actually volunteered for this. August said I should tell you why I'm driving you across the state chasing a lead on a missing girl I don't even know," Max said.

That got Chase's interest. "I figured you all thought this was some real white knight nonsense, but don't you think it's important? Don't you feel like if we don't find her, no one will?"

"I think you'd be better off asking the sheriff to find her."

"If you believed that, you wouldn't have asked to come on this trip. So now I am curious," Chase said. He turned towards Max, giving him his undivided attention.

"Cool, man, that's what I'm getting to. Anyway, give me a second . . . 600,000 people go missing every year. That's a crazy number, but about 6,000 of them are never found."

"You sound like Stefan. How do you know this?"

"Those stats are straight out of a nonprofit my wife and I donate to. Look, everybody's got a thing they don't really talk about. Mine is my neighbor. She would watch us after school. A cute girl who vanished one day, and I remember it felt like no one really cared. It destroyed that family. She watched my siblings and me every day after school. For years. And then one day she just wasn't there, and no one knew what happened. You don't forget that."

"I'm sorry."

"Everyone put up flyers. We joined a big group walking fields around the area looking for her. However, it didn't take long for the interest to fade. In no time at all, it was like she had never existed. She had basically been part of our family, and then she was forgotten."

"I think I get it. I get it, Max."

The two sat in silence for a mile or two before Max spoke up again. "Why are we driving to Snyder?"

"Because neither of us had anybody. Did you know her mom died when she was in college?" Chase didn't wait for an answer. "Car accident her freshman year. She was an only child like me. She never knew her dad and was just suddenly alone in the world."

Chase continued, "Do you think a girl like her lands on a guy like me without some trauma?" He laughed to lighten the mood. That got a laugh out of Max as well.

"And now here we come to save the day, right?"

"I guess I hope so."

* * *

It felt like the whole town of Snyder could fit in its coliseum, which had an actual capacity of just under four thousand. The multiday event included bull riding, saddle bronc riding, bareback riding, steer wrestling, calf roping, breakaway roping, team roping, and barrel racing. But Chase and Max were only there to see if they spotted Tacy.

The roster for Tacy's old team was easy to find on the internet. So were the names of everyone she had competed against, and may have been friends with, from other schools. Diego was already hard at work searching social media. He called to relay that he was deep enough into each name to know that Tacy hadn't popped up on any of their social media accounts.

When the two arrived, they cruised the parking lot looking for Tacy's truck. There was no sign of it. They then entered the coliseum, grabbed beers and hot dogs, and found a couple of seats. They spent the whole night watching the crowd, competitors, and occasionally the events themselves. It turned

71

out they both shared a high tolerance for nachos and pretzels.

At the end of the night, they went out to where the competitors loaded their trailers and asked about Tacy. Plenty of people seemed interested, but no one had actually seen her. Once they were satisfied they had talked to everyone, they filed over to a motel room.

12

Tablelands

Max liked motels with no hallways. He could see the car from the room. Such motels usually had a free breakfast too. The next morning, after Max got his free breakfast, the two were on the campus of W. R. Scurry College. It was home to a golf course with a pro shop which sat next to the building that housed the athletics staff. Max parked in an empty space next to maybe the only golfer preparing to play a round that cold winter morning.

Inside the athletics building, they quickly found office 113.B, which the school's website said would belong to Coach Lyle Hoffman. The space on the door for a nametag was blank, and Chase opened the door assuming the space inside would be much larger than it was. He was met with the surprised look of a young man seated at a desk in the modest, maybe even cramped, room.

"Can I help you?" the young man asked. A W. R. Scurry lanyard hung around his neck and held an employee ID card that Chase couldn't make out. Maybe this was the office of a graduate assistant or a young coach. This wasn't the man pictured on the website as the school's rodeo coach.

"Oh, sorry. I was looking for Coach Hoffman."

"Coach Hoffman? Lyle? You're not going to catch him in an office. You'll need to try his mobile . . . I can probably find that number for you if you need it."

Chase already had the coach's phone number from the same website roster that listed his office address. "I've got it. Sorry to interrupt. Have a good one."

"No problem. Have a good day, sir."

The two exited the building. Chase was already dialing his phone. He wasn't surprised to encounter the typical West Texas politeness on the other end of the call. "Call me Lyle," the coach said.

Chase explained that he was in town looking for his missing girlfriend. It had only been a couple of years since Lyle coached Tacy. "You were asking around about her last night? I heard about that. I haven't really kept in touch with her, much less seen her. However, I'm happy to help. What can I do for you?"

"Where'd she learn to ride?" Chase asked.

"Right here. Tacy's roommate her first year was on the team and worked with her out at a ranch north of Fluvanna," he said. Tablelands Guest Ranch, as he described it, was a dude ranch where people could vacation and ride horses.

According to Lyle, Tacy was immediately horse crazy and started practicing with the team shortly after the fall semester started. But her first year was "frankly, not great."

"She just didn't have a background with horses, and even with extra help from her teammates, she needed time to figure out the sport. She was just starting to be competitive when her mom died."

There was a crackle that made Coach Lyle hard to hear at times, but Chase could hear well enough to follow along. "She was liked by everyone. We all leaned in to help her after her mom died, but you had to pull information out of her. She genuinely loved horses, but she kept people at a certain distance."

"Even with her roommate? The one she worked with at Tablelands?"

"Shy-Anne Mayfield. Her family owns Tablelands. The family moved out from the Austin area when they bought the place. I got the sense they had more money than God, but I don't actually know the family, and Shy-Anne hasn't kept in touch."

He went on to explain that Tacy had borrowed a horse from Tablelands during her time at W. R. Scurry. The two-year college, named after a Republic of Texas politician, was largely attended by local kids who continued to four-year schools after graduation.

"Graduation comes fast around here," the coach said. He lamented the constant turnover of new faces and how little time they all had together.

"Sounds like if she was going to be in touch with someone it would be at Tablelands," Chase said.

"Absolutely," said the coach.

Feeling good about the call, Chase had Max relay everything about Shy-Anne and Tablelands to Diego. He confirmed she was on the team roster he had, but she had no social media presence at all. Max suggested they put some effort into trying to find out more about her.

* * *

Just an hour south of Lubbock sat the Tablelands Guest Ranch.

It was home to an intermittent stream that, in a wet year, could lazily work its way east to one of the forks of the mighty Brazos River. Diego relayed that the ranch's website boasted a "once in a lifetime western vacation experience" and said guests had the chance to work alongside staff on a real horse ranch.

According to property records, the Mayfield family bought 948 acres, an average operation for this area. A search of county clerk records showed the family also had leases on surrounding places allowing them to engage in "agritourism," which Diego said was probably trail rides for guests.

Turning off US-84 near Justiceburg, the pair drove another fifteen minutes before turning off the highway into an impressive front gate. Towering over the road was a welded steel sign made of one-foot-tall letters proclaiming this to be Tablelands Guest Ranch.

A well-kept pipe fence lined both sides of the road all the way to the sprawling ranch complex. Even from what felt like a great distance, Chase could see a large open arena connected to a horse barn, another barn with hay visible through the open door, a distinctive green John Deere tractor being driven out of a third barn, and at least two bunkhouses with several cars parked outside of each.

The buildings sprawled out in front of them sat left to right in a straight line. As they got closer, Chase could see that each building was clearly marked with signage to direct guests where to park. The ranch was busy with horses and riders occupying the arena and various cowboy-hat-and-jeans-clad men and women walking around. It was a busy morning.

The road fed them into the center of the campus and forced Max to decide between turning left or right. Both ways would lead them alongside the front of the buildings. As the decision approached, Max slowed his vehicle to reduce the cloud of dust following behind the SUV.

The sign for Guest Registration encouraged them to go left. Aside from rows of evergreens planted to slow the unrelenting wind, tall trees were at a premium in this part of the state. One tree, probably a welcome relief from the sun in summer months, narrowed the driveway enough to force Max to slow even further. As he drove past it, a woman on horseback approached his vehicle from the next building down. The rising sun sat behind her, making it impossible to tell much about her beyond some blonde hair sticking out from under her cowboy hat.

Max brought the SUV to a stop and rolled his window down. Chase couldn't see the rider from the passenger seat.

"Can I help you?" she asked. She sounded young.

"I'm Max Gruber . . . I have Chase here with me."

The rider didn't respond.

"We just came from seeing Coach Hoffman at Scurry," Max said.

"Oh . . . Coach Lyle sent you?" she responded after a slight pause.

"You bet," Max said.

Must be Shy-Anne, Chase thought.

"You can park your car over there," she said. Chase still couldn't see her face, but he could see her arm point to an empty space in front of the closest building. As Max rolled up his window and started to pull away, she yelled, "Hold tight at your car and I'll come back out to get you!"

Once Max's window was rolled up he turned to Chase and practically yelled, "That's Tacy!"

"What are you talking about?" Chase opened the SUV door,

forcing Max to slam on the brakes, which ripped the door out of Chase's hand. He stepped out just as the young rider was starting to turn the corner and almost out of sight. He poked his head back in the Explorer. "No. That was absolutely not Tacy. Not even a little bit. What is your problem?"

Max sat with wide eyes, raised eyebrows, and an open mouth until Chase let him off the hook with a laugh.

The two stood outside the SUV as Chase gave Max a hard time for "thinking all blondes on horseback look the same" and telling him that he'd "be a terrible private investigator."

Eventually, the young cowgirl returned on foot.

"I'm Max Gruber," Max said as he extended his hand.

"Shy-Anne Mayfield," she said, returning the handshake.

"Chase Haven," Chase said, also extending his hand.

"Wait . . . Who?"

"Tacy's boyfriend," Chase said.

"*The* Chase Haven?" Shy-Anne asked.

"I guess." He couldn't contain a smile.

Shy-Anne told them all about her time with Tacy in college, how she taught her to ride, and how she gave Tacy everything she needed for breakaway roping.

Chase unloaded all of his thoughts. He filled Shy-Anne in on every detail he could think of. He started from the beginning. Finally, he asked the most obvious question.

"Have you seen her?"

"I haven't seen her, but that isn't unusual. She's done a holiday or two with us. We call on birthdays. She called when she got fired. I asked her to come back here, but she said she was in love."

Love? Chase thought. He hadn't heard that word from Tacy and he was sucker punched by a flood of emotion.

Shy-Anne, pausing only occasionally to greet people as they walked past, continued the conversation. "If Tacy was headed anywhere, it would be here. She loved horses more than rodeos." She briefly asked a passing cowboy to square away a horse for a guest coming off a ride before turning back to the men. "Tacy said her job had been like the lunch tables in high school."

"How so?" Max asked.

"The jocks, band, and theater kids eat lunch at their own separate tables. In small towns, everyone is aligned in their groups the same way. We've seen it firsthand, and it isn't something you see in a big city. You can't ever be invisible or anonymous in a small town. Whatever lunch table you sit at follows you through every interaction in town," Shy-Anne said.

"I get it, but the tables are families, and those families don't solve disagreements with a food fight," Chase said.

"No, small towns solve their disagreements quietly, right? And it isn't enough to have all the same friends as everyone in your group. You must also share the same enemies."

"Right. If my friends don't like you, I don't like you. Tacy saw that in action," Chase said.

Shy-Anne shared her contact information once it was clear they had exchanged as much information as they had. As Chase and Max drove the three hours back to Horsehead Crossing, Chase couldn't help but be discouraged. Something was wrong.

As they pulled back into town, he was reminded of how Stefan said the famous cattleman Charles Goodnight once described the area: "The graveyard of the cowman's hopes." He wasn't feeling especially hopeful at the moment himself.

13

Canutillo

Between the conversations with Max on their drive to Snyder and Tablelands and answering questions for Diego who was searching the internet, Chase felt like he had assembled a small biography of Tacy. However, it had some big holes.

Tacy had been something of a nomad. Raised by a single mom, the two had moved around a few times. All Chase knew was that Tacy had graduated from a high school in a suburb of El Paso. He talked Max into extending their trip to check it out.

The two found themselves at the only motel in Anthony, Texas. The little town sat on the New Mexico border just outside El Paso and Franklin Mountains State Park. The two had spent their morning hiking to the top of North Franklin Mountain, a 7,100-foot peak that took almost five hours to hike. That hike, which Tacy had once joked was "the twenty-seventh highest peak in Texas," was the only thing she had ever mentioned about the place.

"Well, most people don't know there are any mountains in Texas, much less twenty-seven of them," Chase joked to Max. Chase appreciated that Max hadn't questioned him about the pointless detour up the trail. It wouldn't do anything to find Tacy, but Chase wanted to see it.

By the time they finished the hike, a bundle of information they had asked Diego to gather was ready. Diego had really outdone himself with his research on Tacy's hometown, but he couldn't figure out who Tacy's father might be or where he was. It looked like he was out of the picture from the start of her life, because the birth certificate Diego produced for Tacy didn't list a father.

Diego confirmed that Tacy graduated from high school in Canutillo, which was crammed between Anthony and the growing city of El Paso. Her mother worked at an outlet mall on Interstate 10, and they lived alone in town.

Additionally, they had moved around a lot. The birth certificate was from Beaumont, an industrial town in southeast Texas. Her mom also popped up in Bishop outside of Corpus Christi on the Gulf Coast as well as Tyler in the Piney Woods of East Texas.

Getting any time from Diego was a big deal, and in just one morning he had supplied them with enough information to justify their trip to Tacy's hometown. He would just laugh when Chase asked him how he collected his information. If Chase pressed, he'd just say, "the internet."

Their first stop was a maze of manufactured homes. Once they hit the intersection of Road C and C Street, Chase knew this had to be the least creative mobile home park on earth. Road A, Road B, A Street, and B Street also snaked their way through the neighborhood. Chase had called the office for the mobile home park, but the woman who answered had never heard of Tacy Vernon or her mother.

Once they arrived at her old address, the For Rent sign in the yard drilled home the fact that residents in the area may not put down roots for very long. Sure enough, the few people they stopped to ask had never heard of a Tacy Vernon. This was a waste of time.

Their stop at Tacy's old high school was also uneventful. Chase walked in the door of the school office well after the last bell, when he was sure all the kids had left and staff would be most open to a chat. However, the three ladies inside the office were of no help.

The school had almost four hundred kids in each grade and a front office staff that wasn't up for answering questions. Chase's claim to be writing for a rodeo magazine didn't help to get them talking. They referred him to their communications team and sent him on his way.

The two also checked out the outlet mall on the interstate, but the store Diego said her mother had worked at was no longer in business. Not feeling especially productive, the two called August.

"Diego said you're wasting your time out there. He specifically said you're wasting *his* time," August said.

"Feels like it," Chase said.

"Then do me a favor. Give Stefan a call on your way back. Like I said, you need him involved in this."

* * *

"You're on speaker with Max," Chase said.

"You two still in Snyder?" Stefan asked.

"No, we talked to her old coach, found her old roommate outside of Fluvanna, and then wasted a day in her old hometown," Chase said.

82

"Where's that?" Stefan asked.

"El Paso. Point is, she hasn't reconnected with anyone," Chase said.

"Well, no one has seen her here, but she's come up on Facebook since you left," Stefan said.

"How so?" Max asked.

"Somebody complained on the city's Facebook page about Turner Cam's 'too stupid to understand the airport' comment. The whole town has chimed in on it. That's all anyone is talking about."

"That was like a month ago," Chase said.

"Yeah, well, it's new information to everyone on Facebook, and now they're rehashing every issue the city has ever had. Bad roads, bad drinking water, and everyone has an opinion on firing Tacy."

"I'll check it out. You going to the meeting tomorrow?" Chase asked.

"Yeah, I'll be there," Stefan said.

14

The Patrons

The Patrons sat two blocks off the square and was available for private parties at a reasonable rate. It was not only an often-used building for events, but it was also a social organization. The American Society of the Patrons of Husbandry met once a week for lunch.

Technically the oldest agriculture advocacy group in the United States, the local meeting of the Patrons had turned into an hour of camaraderie and networking for business owners and local politicians. Chase always sat in the same spot at what Stefan jokingly called "the Lutheran Table." He was joined by several stalwart church leaders, the same regulars as the weekly breakfast.

Stefan was already at the Lutheran Table when Chase arrived. He rose to shake hands. Stefan then leaned over and whispered, "Do you see what's on the menu today?"

"Lord, no," Chase said. He immediately knew that it must be the King Ranch Casserole made with tuna instead of chicken. They both privately complained about it, but no one would dare share their feedback with the young couple who made the meals. It was assumed the two were struggling to get their catering business off the ground. Their normally stellar food was served in an unpredictable rotation, making it difficult to skip the monthly appearance of this seafood version of the classic Tex-Mex dish.

"We've made a terrible mistake," Stefan whispered. Chase couldn't help but laugh in response.

After most of the meals were consumed, or at least pushed around the plate, Mayor Turner Cam rose to address the group. He was in a blue polo shirt embroidered with a ram's head appearing over the letters ASU, the logo for the Angelo State University Rams. As he stood before the crowd waiting for them to notice his presence and organically end their conversations, he motioned for Aaron Foster to join him.

Aaron Foster was in cotton khaki slacks and a solid navy tie. The two stood together as Turner began to speak. "I just wanted to take a moment to let Aaron talk to y'all about a very important topic. I'd appreciate it if you gave him your attention. There's been a lot of miscommunication going around about what's going on up at the airport. We've got an opportunity to do a lot of good for the community if some of the naysayers could just educate themselves about the airport."

He continued by detailing the history of the airport, which was built by the US Army Corps of Engineers in 1942 to train pilots for the US Army Air Forces. Similar facilities were built in the counties of Gray, Ward, and elsewhere. After the war, the county took over ownership of the field, and it was used almost exclusively by a Fortune 500 oil and gas conglomerate, which owned an 8,000-acre property nearby. Executives, clients, and politicians had been flown in for guided hunts for almost thirty years. No one could recall whether it was a change in company leadership or just tough economic times that caused the company to sell their property and stop the regular flights.

The county had then voted to close the underused airport. That's when city leaders took ownership of it. Turner Cam, who was still working his way through his lengthy introduction, pivoted to a tour of the facility he was invited to the previous weekend.

Not one to shy away from namedropping, he mentioned that he had spent his Saturday with Baxter Whitey at his invitation. He learned some pilot slang and detailed how Baxter had taken him for a "$100 hamburger." This was when pilots fly to another destination just to eat lunch—the $100 signifying the cost of operating the plane, not the actual cost of the meal. The mayor had stressed that the airport was home to a very active group of pilots who had both personal and professional interests in the airport.

While Baxter had never attended a meeting of the Patrons, the mayor still made sure to connect the influential man to the airport project before introducing Aaron Foster. "I'd like our city manager and airport administrator to walk you through this project he's working on. It is the single most important project of my three terms as mayor."

Aaron Foster, without the aid of handouts or a projector, proceeded to read the same presentation he had given the EDC. His words came out one at a time, like he had to analyze each one before spitting it from his mouth. He read every word with his eyes glued to the paper in his hand. He completely ignored the audience until he turned the page to his financial spreadsheet.

Everyone, except Aaron himself, realized that he had lost his audience. He was cut off by the mayor, who appeared to be turning his predictable red, likely angered by Aaron boring the important audience.

By the next day, the entire town had heard about what happened next. Rumors of it spread like wildfire through the community. Each retelling came with a custom hypothesis and universal disappointment to have "missed the show."

"While Aaron was speaking, I looked over at this bowl of candy on each table," Turner said. He took a step to the bowl at the nearest table and grabbed a couple of pieces and held them up to the crowd, who were now very much paying attention. "Smarties and Dum Dums. That's what we've got showing up to city council meetings and going on Facebook with nothing but complaints."

"Smarties and Dum Dums!" He raised his voice and threw the candy to the ground. The roll of Smarties exploded in a cloud of candy fragments and sugary dust. A Dum Dum slid across the floor towards Chase, almost striking his foot.

Chase sat with his hands clinched in fists.

"We've got people doing their dead-level best day and night to make this the best place on earth to live. That's all undone by a handful of people. Just a few who yell louder than the rest. People who never have anything good to say. All we get is hate spewed at us on Facebook," he said. The crowd was frozen in their seats.

"We don't have any money to fix the streets, which is why we need this airport. But how do we compete with lies? Most of which are spread over at that no-good Lutheran breakfast," he said. He looked directly at the Lutheran Table. They all sat in shock, mouths agape. The crowd was too startled to respond to the sudden and unexpected turn in the presentation.

"And those no-good newcomers. Carpetbaggers. They come

from Dallas and Austin and think they can buy the whole place."

The mayor then attacked the "no-good radio station."

Chase stood. The crowd, still frozen, watched as the mayor walked right out the door in midsentence. In fact, many would later describe it as a crabwalk. He shuffled sideways out of the door in a way every bit as peculiar as the rant itself. It was as if he was flanking his own words, which he had just left hanging in the air. He left everyone in stunned silence staring at the door and then at each other.

The crowd had not begun to move, much less speak, except for Chase. He was out the door and hot on the heels of Turner Cam.

15

Whip

Chase was out the door before anyone could stop him. Turner
Cam had made it to his car, his hand on the door. Chase took
him by surprise. He grabbed the mayor's collar from behind
in a firm grip and pulled back as he drove his foot forward into
the back of the man's knee. The mayor crumpled to the ground.
It was an unnatural movement. He grabbed his leg and rolled
on the ground screaming in pain.

Chase stood over him considering his next move when he was
tackled from behind. He tried his best to catch himself, but he
fell face down on the gravel driveway and had to fight to turn
over and face his attacker. It was Whip. He stopped.

He was face-to-face with Sheriff Winthorp "Whip" Dantonio.
A regular at these lunches, the sight of the sheriff hit Chase like
cold water. He raised his hands. "It's cool! I'm cool!"

"Roll over and put your hands behind your back," Whip said.

Chase complied. His wrists were quickly wrenched away, and
he felt the snap of handcuffs.

Whip rolled Chase onto his side and helped him to his feet.
He then spoke into the radio on his collar. Chase couldn't even

hear what he said. Everything was moving too fast.

All the town's leaders were on the porch watching the spectacle. From that crowd came August's voice, the first voice Chase heard clearly from the sea of noise around him.

"Why is Chase in cuffs? The mayor was a danger. He needed to be stopped," August said.

Then Stefan chimed in, "He had some sort of meltdown. He was in no condition to drive."

The mayor didn't respond, but he did try to get up. He tried to leave. But he couldn't. He collapsed back onto the ground and leaned against his car. No one approached him as he sat alone grasping his knee.

Whip put Chase in the back of his cruiser and then checked on Turner. Chase couldn't hear what was said, but the crowd was freely talking amongst themselves and even to Whip.

An ambulance finally arrived. Once Turner was en route to the hospital, something which did not entice the crowd to leave, Whip drove Chase to the sheriff's station.

Chase kept his head down during the drive. For the first time he felt the palms of his hands, which burned from the hard landing on the gravel parking lot.

It was a short trip. Whip parked directly next to the door.

"You were read your rights, correct?" Whip asked. He helped Chase out of the cruiser.

"Yeah, *you* read them to me," Chase said. Whip opened the station door and propped it open with his foot.

"I want to make sure you understand them. Do you?" Whip led Chase inside.

"Yes, sir." As Chase answered, he saw Corely standing at a long desk that spanned most of the front room of the station. A deputy was on the other side. Their conversation stopped when the two appeared.

Corely turned and saw Chase as they entered. "What is going on?" she asked.

"Probably best you ask Stefan," Chase said. He tilted his head towards the sheriff.

"Is Stefan okay?" A worried look crossed her face.

"He's fine. Eating lunch at the Patrons. This is a me thing. He can fill you in."

She was typing something, probably Stefan's contact, on her phone as she walked past the two and into the parking lot.

Whip sat Chase in a small room. It was an austere space. Just chairs and a small table. Whip removed his handcuffs.

"For now, you sit. Maybe for a good bit. I'm going to do some paperwork, ask you for a statement, and then probably do some more paperwork." Whip walked towards the door. As he did, a deputy stepped into the doorway, handed Whip a piece of paper, and left.

Chase cleared his throat. "I don't have anything to say."

"You sure?" Whip stopped reading what was placed in his hand and turned back to face Chase.

"Yeah. I'm not answering any questions."

Whip walked back to the table, pulled out the chair opposite Chase, and sat down. "Okay." He took a small tape recorder out of his pocket, set it on the table, and turned it on. A little red light lit up, indicating it was recording. "Then how about you tell me about this missing girlfriend of yours?"

Chase leaned forward in his chair. "Tacy quit at that city council meeting. Instead of going home, she drove out of town. No one has seen or talked to her since."

"The whole town heard about that meeting. Corely Beldame filed this request to locate today. Why didn't you file that report yourself?" Whip held up the paper in his hand.

"A missing person's report?"

"No. A missing person's report is when we suspect foul play. It's a request to locate when a young girl just needs a break from her boyfriend."

Chase was mad, but he tried not to let it show. He waited a moment before replying. "She found a lot of problems over at the city. Financial issues with the airport. She was going to blow the whistle."

"Blow the whistle?"

"Yes, she had enough dirt. I saw it. It was real."

"What do you suspect, then?"

Chase leaned back in his chair. "I don't know."

"No theory? Then why didn't you report her missing?"

Chase was about to say they'd had a fight, but he stopped himself. "I asked Corely to do it. We talked about this a lot. We weren't sure what to do. We all agreed to do it. Stefan too."

"I think you thought she'd had enough of this place, went back home or to be with friends. She used to rodeo. She might be following the circuit. Maybe she's traveling around with an old boyfriend. Doing rodeo stuff together."

Chase was too angry to respond.

"Okay, let's start from the beginning." Whip then asked Chase about the night Tacy disappeared. Chase told him about the city council meeting, watching Tacy leave, driving out to look for her, and going to her house.

"People saw you at the city council meeting?"

"Yes."

"And would anyone have seen you driving out to find her or going to her house?"

"Probably not."

"When was the next time someone saw you?"

"I went to the Butterfield the next night."

"So, no one saw you for twenty-four hours?"

"I don't know. I guess not."

"The twenty-four hours during which your girlfriend goes missing, and you don't run into anyone?"

"I didn't really leave my apartment."

"Why not? Did you two have a fight or something? Or did you already know where she was?"

Chase shook his head. For a quick second he almost felt the urge to cry, which didn't make sense and just made him angrier. He looked down at his hands covered in small cuts from the driveway. They had quieted to a dull, vibrating pain that seemed to match his heart rate.

"We're going to find her. When we do, I won't shy away from charging you with obstruction for lying to me. It will pair nicely with the assault charge. I don't buy that you were stopping the mayor from driving."

Chase didn't reply. He had just enough command of his emotions to bite his tongue.

Whip stood and walked to the door. He turned to Chase as he left. "Don't go anywhere."

Chase sat staring blankly ahead. Time was still moving briskly. His head was swimming. It felt like minutes before Whip returned, but it had been much longer than that. He stood in the doorway.

"Okay, Romeo. The mayor called the county attorney and asked that we not press charges. He didn't strike me as a fan of yours, though."

"He isn't a fan," Chase said. He stared at the wall instead of the sheriff.

"The mayor had a medical episode. Says that he hasn't felt right since an accident the other night."

Chase's eyes shot back to the sheriff. "What accident?"

"News to me, but I don't get briefed on every little thing. A city truck burned up. We responded, but there was nothing for us to do. He didn't go to the hospital or anything. The fire department put it out. Pretty routine."

"When was this?"

"After the city council meeting, while you were running around without being seen by anyone. A city crew left some chemicals in the bed of the truck or something. Whole thing went up like a Roman candle."

"What's the mayor doing driving a city truck around late at night?"

"He wasn't driving."

"Then who was?"

Whip just stared back, silent.

"Aaron Foster?"

Whip's expression changed to a sneer.

"It *was* Aaron Foster!" Chase said. "Those two are just cruising around in a city truck and it catches on fire?"

Whip didn't react.

"Am I free to go?"

Whip put his hand on his hips. "It doesn't work like that. What happens to you is my decision."

"But I can go?" Chase held his hands out, palms up, as if he was still in handcuffs.

"I'm going to take everyone's statements, see how injured the mayor turns out to be, and then chat with the county attorney."

"He decides? The county attorney?"

"I'll forward what I have to him, a warrant will be issued, and you'll be back in here."

"How long until the county attorney decides?"

"Whenever he pleases. Two years if he wants to."

Chase thought about having this hang over his head for two years.

"Our time together tonight isn't quite done." Whip returned to the chair opposite Chase. He repeated his questions about Tacy for another thirty minutes. Finally, he stood. "You should expect to be back in here. In cuffs again. But you're free to go for now."

Whip left the room. Chase followed him out and then turned and exited to the parking lot. He called Stefan. At first, he wanted a ride home, but it dawned on him how long it would take Stefan to get into town. He could walk home by then. He briefed his friend on everything that happened while he walked.

Chase was sure he wouldn't get any sleep, not with thoughts of the city truck burning, Tacy running off with an old boyfriend, and finding himself in prison racing through his mind. However, he passed out the minute he sat on his couch. He didn't even make it to bed.

16

Same Page

A fresh copy of the newspaper sat at the Butterfield waiting for Chase the next morning. It was folded so that he could only see the top half of the front page. He felt some relief when it didn't appear to mention anything about the airport or Tacy. No way it could mention the mayor's meltdown considering the paper likely went to print before that even happened. His feeling of relief didn't last beyond him flipping the paper over to see that the lower half of the front page was dedicated to the airport.

"Sky High Rumors: Airport Decries Fake News"

"Gosh," he said to himself, "this is going to be ridiculous."

The entire article cited only one source, Aaron Foster, and it made sure to repeatedly credit the city manager with running a successful airport. The writer started by "debunking" the recent radio interview without going so far as to name Tacy. However, he didn't address any of her claims directly. Instead, the article stated that the airport was profitable, that criticism was from people who didn't understand the complicated airport budget, and that their finances were regularly audited.

"Auditors aren't trained to detect fraud," Stefan said. He had walked in without Chase noticing. "Read it this morning." He patted Chase on the shoulder and then took a seat next to him. He sat quietly, giving Chase a chance to finish reading.

The second half of the article, which took up most of an entire page deeper in the paper, focused on the "hundreds of thousands" of dollars the airport contributed to the local economy each year. It didn't mention Baxter Whitey. Instead, it mentioned that many local pilots used the airport for business and pleasure. It also recounted the history of the airport and how users were optimistic that expanding the facility would continue to grow the local economy.

It looked like every point from Aaron Foster's airport hangar proposal had been repeated in the article. The airport was an undeniable economic engine, the expansion was a much-needed boost for the stagnant local economy, and everyone who questioned the project didn't understand it.

"I guess we're both too stupid to understand the airport," Chase joked although he wasn't in a joking mood.

Stefan was about to reply when Chase's phone began to vibrate audibly on the table. The caller ID read "TCAM." He briefly turned it to face Stefan. "This will be fun," he said as he put the phone up to his ear.

"Hey, Chase. How's it going?" asked Turner Cam.

Chase didn't bite. No fake politeness today. "What can I do for you?" Strictly business.

"I wanted to thank you for keeping me off the roads yesterday. I don't remember anything from the event, but doctors called it hypoglycemic rage. I was in dire need of medical attention. I'm told that you could have saved my life and the lives of others."

"Really?" There was more than enough sarcasm in his voice.

"I'm moving slowly, but already back to work."

Chase wasn't immediately sure how to respond. Turner Cam spoke as if he hadn't lost his mind in front of the town's most connected leaders just twenty hours before.

"I saw the paper today," Chase finally said.

"It lays it all out. I worked with them on it, and it is all facts. I know Tacy got turned around on this whole thing. I haven't had a chance to talk to her about it," Turner said.

How dare he even say her name. Was the burned-out city truck a coincidence? Chase thought about beating some facts out of the mayor, but he had to be smarter than that. He couldn't find Tacy from behind bars.

"The project loses money," Chase said. He was willing to join the mayor in pretending he wasn't the talk of the town this morning, but he wasn't willing to let the airport stuff that Tacy researched be summarized like that.

"Not the numbers I'm looking at. Maybe you have some outdated figures. The current presentation . . . it looks good. Could I take a look at what you've got? I'd hate for you to go down a rabbit hole with something that was never meant to go to the public."

"Mayor, these are the figures that went to the EDC. These are the figures you took to them yourself."

Then an entirely new and unexpected voice joined the call. "Those are good numbers. The numbers are good."

Chase didn't respond. *Sounds like someone else who needs some facts beat out of them*, he thought.

"This is Aaron Foster here, Chase. I just walked in the door and the mayor waved me over. If you two are talking about the airport, I'd like to help you on that."

"Tacy laid it all out. This doesn't even cover the cost of the loan, but you also have other financial problems out there,"

Chase said.

"If I could just take a look at what you have, maybe we could sort all of this out," Turner said.

Chase spoke more for Stefan's benefit than the mayor or city manager. "You want me to bring you everything Tacy has on the airport and the other projects?"

Stefan shot him a puzzled look.

"That'd help us get on the same page," Turner said.

"When?" Chase asked.

"We're free after lunch," Aaron said.

"Fine. After lunch then. City hall at 1. Thank you both for your service." It felt like something the mayor would say. Chase hung up without waiting for a reply.

Stefan smiled. "What in the world do you have cooking?"

"I need a printer. We've got work to do." Chase stood. Stefan followed his lead.

"I'll tell you everything once we get to my place."

17

110 Nights

Chase pulled up to city hall to the sight of Aaron Foster standing next to a white pickup on the curb in front of the door. He had on a white short-sleeve Oxford shirt, a solid blue tie, and khaki slacks. The outfit was solidly within his predictable range of attire.

Chase stepped out of his truck. He had half a ream of paper, still warm from his printer, in a folder in his hand.

"Good afternoon," the city manager said.

Chase thought about punching him in his mouth. Instead, he replied, "Afternoon. How are you?"

"Fine." Aaron walked to the driver's door of the city truck. "Shall we?"

Chase settled into the passenger seat of the truck without a question. The bare interior was no frills. No air conditioning or radio. The windows were rolled down. They were mechanical— the type Chase had called "roll 'em up windows" as a kid.

"No mayor?" Chase looked across to Aaron.

"He's not feeling well. I thought we'd do a quick tour of town," Aaron said. He went on to call their drive the "real"

100

introduction to the city.

The two drove around for about thirty minutes. Aaron would occasionally slow down to point out an especially bad patch of concrete. There were many.

"We're the only town that does these repairs ourselves?" Chase asked.

"Other towns hire this out. Our crews can do it cheaper in-house."

"And the other towns can't do the same?"

"No, they don't run a street crew like I do," Aaron said. He turned onto a street actively being worked on. Two city trucks, both clearly newer and more fully featured than the one they were in, were several feet apart on the residential street. Three men were working in front of one of the trucks. Armed with a shovel, broom, and bags of cold mix, the three cleaned debris from a pothole and then filled it with the bag of material. A fourth employee drove the second truck over a freshly filled pothole, using the weight of it to flatten and smooth the repair.

Aaron stopped the truck several feet away and described all of these steps. This took several minutes until he finally pulled the truck closer to the three men. As Aaron leaned out of his window to address the men, they paused their work but made no effort to approach the truck. The fourth continued driving over freshly patched potholes, ignoring the arrival of the city manager.

"Taking this one on a tour around town," he said. The three nodded towards Chase, who raised his hand in a static wave in reply. "I told him why we do this work in-house. That's how you keep your jobs. Even if people in town complain about the streets."

Chase couldn't see Aaron's eyes, but it looked like he had

slightly turned his head toward Chase, as if to signal to them that he was critical of their work.

"We're working real hard out here, Mr. Foster. We appreciate all that you do for us," one said.

A closed-mouth smile spread across Aaron Foster's face. He didn't reply, but instead drove off. Headed to the town's treatment plant, Aaron shifted the conversation to the town's water needs. He estimated that a combined $100 million in repairs to water pipes, sewer lines, and streets were necessary.

"Where are we going to get that money?" Chase asked.

"We aren't without new revenue . . . like growing the airport." The smile reappeared. It was really more of a smirk.

"What we do here is complicated. The crew all have certifications. The state's out here making sure we do things correctly," Aaron said. The two pulled up to the locked gate of the facility.

"Is that why they keep making you issue boil water notices? People have to boil their water because you're doing such a good job?" Chase asked.

"I'll try to explain, but you don't have the training or certifications we have," Aaron said. He stepped out of the truck and unlocked the security gate. He returned to the truck and pulled it up to the facility itself.

Once inside, Aaron seemed intent on dragging out the tour in order to explain everything to Chase in childlike detail. Chase decided to lean into it. He began asking questions himself.

"What's this?" Chase asked. He pointed to a large metal housing bolted to the ground. He had no idea what it was.

"A pump."

"How'd you go about selecting this model?"

"An engineering firm. They calculated what we needed."

"But you put it in?"

"No, that's not something a treatment plant operator would do."

"And the routine maintenance? You do that?"

"No. We don't have the staff for that. We schedule that and keep the records. It is very complex machinery."

"Your certifications don't cover this type of work?"

"Our certifications cover the daily operation, which is very specialized."

"Got it."

Aaron had been much more talkative than in any public setting in which Chase had seen him, but the juvenile back-and-forth cooled off their conversation a great bit. They drove to their next destination, the airport, in silence.

Once the two turned into the main entrance, Aaron was using all his words again.

"Did you know that airport visitors book 110 nights in local motels every year?"

Impressive recall memory, Chase thought to himself as Aaron became more verbose.

"They spend $22,400 per year at local restaurants."

Was he reading this? He was! He had to be. Aaron kept looking down at his left hand, tucked between his seat and the door of the truck. Chase was sure he had these facts written down just out of sight.

"Plus $15,000 spent in miscellaneous expenses in town."

"That's great . . . I don't have anything against the airport itself—just the new project."

"The new project *is* the airport. You seem to be right there with the primary opponents to that."

"Well, okay, how about you show me how this place works?" Chase suggested.

The next hour was spent walking the existing facilities including hangars, the under-construction pilots' lounge, and the refueling area.

The two got back in the truck.

"Each time you see the shadow of a plane overhead, that's money coming to town. What do you think of that?" Aaron asked. He was really using up all his words today.

"The airport reminds me of the ostriches."

"Ostriches?"

"Yeah, when people thought raising ostriches was going to make them rich, but instead it bankrupted them. They had some pretty impressive financial projections too, I bet," Chase said. Any smirk on Aaron Foster's face was now a distant memory.

They drove back to city hall in silence.

Once back, Chase followed Aaron to his office. No sign of the mayor. Chase took a seat. He eyed the bookshelves that lined the wall behind Aaron.

"Can I see what you brought?" Aaron asked. He was eyeing the folder of papers Chase had brought with him.

"You bet, but I'm curious about the wall behind you full of files. None of them are labeled. What's up with that?"

"They're what you've been told they are," Aaron said.

"Where's your file on Tacy Vernon?"

Aaron's eyes did not shoot over to the wall of folders behind him. Instead, they went to a folder sitting on his desk. He caught himself and looked back to Chase. "Why her?"

"She's missing. Do you know where she is?"

Aaron slammed a fist into his desk. "How would I know about that?!"

City hall fell silent instantly. Any faint buzzing of activity in the building halted at the outburst.

On the double, he regained his calm. "She doesn't have a file. She was a city employee. These aren't personnel files."

"I heard you kept these files, but I somehow still didn't believe it." Chase stood. "In what realm is this acceptable? Do you understand how crazy this makes you look?"

"Crazy?!" Aaron's fist pounded the desk again.

"You have to know I'm going to hang this around your neck. This is so far out of line I'm—"

"You'll what?" Aaron asked. He stood and stepped around to the side of his desk.

"I'll get busy on some open records requests. Warm up your copy machine," Chase said. He narrowed his eyes as he stared at the still-angry city manager.

"Then get out of my office and get to work."

Chase realized that any file on Tacy would be destroyed or hidden. He had to act now.

"Better yet, I'll stop by to see what the sheriff has to say about you having a vendetta file on a missing person," Chase said.

"Get out!" Aaron yelled. He pointed to the door. "Get out right now!"

"Or . . ." Chase firmly planted both hands in Aaron's chest and pushed him against the bookshelf. He then turned toward the desk and grabbed the file.

As he opened the folder, Aaron grabbed his shoulder. Chase twisted his upper body sharply to shake off Aaron's grip.

The first page was titled "Tacy Vernon."

Aaron was grabbing at Chase again, but Chase shrugged him off and opened his office door. The entire city office staff was in the next room. They were frozen, watching Aaron's door.

Chase ignored them and headed out to the street. Just a few

feet from the door, as he passed the city truck he had spent his day in, a deputy sheriff turned the corner on foot. At the same time, Aaron Foster came barreling out the door.

Chase had a stolen file in his hand. That file might have been his best chance to find Tacy, but he couldn't find her from inside a jail cell. As he made the split-second decision, an immediate sense of regret washed over him.

Chase threw the folder into the open window of the truck. He did it before the deputy raised his eyes and spotted him and the trailing Aaron Foster.

"What's going on?" the deputy asked. "I got a report of a loud argument."

"No sir, just a late water bill. All sorted now," Chase said.

Aaron, seeing the file in the truck, walked around to the driver's door. "All sorted out, but, Deputy, if you have a moment I'd like to ask you a question." Aaron opened the driver's side door and sat behind the wheel, leaning towards the open passenger window and putting his hand over the folder on the seat.

Chase continued walking. He turned his head to watch as the two chatted briefly until Aaron started the truck and drove away.

18

421 Feet

Chase saw that Aaron Foster had turned left. He jumped into his own truck and prepared to do the same. Thankfully, the city manager was stuck at the next light. The city truck's left blinker flashed intermittently.

When the light turned green, the city truck worked its way through the intersection. Chase waited to pull out onto the road so that he wouldn't be spotted by Aaron, but that meant he was caught at the same light as the city truck disappeared down the road.

When the light turned green again, Chase turned and gunned it. His truck was humming loudly as Chase went well over the speed limit and hoped a deputy wasn't sitting in their usual spot on the edge of town.

Foster could have turned off anywhere in town. Chase would have never seen it happen. He gambled that the man was headed out of town.

Chase squinted as he drove in an effort to improve his vision. The afternoon sun was still high, but it looked like a white pickup was ahead of him on the road.

Within another minute he was close enough to increase his confidence that he was behind Aaron Foster's city truck. He didn't dare get any closer. He dialed his phone.

"August, I sure could use your help, and I mean ASAP."

"What's up?"

"I think I need a hand. Can you get it moving towards town while I tell you?"

"My boots are already pointed towards the truck. What's going on?"

"I need to keep my eyes on Aaron Foster, but I can't do it in my truck. I need something he won't recognize."

"Where are you?"

"Following him outside of town on FM 11. He'll spot me for sure in my truck if he hasn't already. I asked him about Tacy, and he lost it. He really does keep files on everyone, and he's either destroying his file on Tacy right now or he's going to go do it soon."

"Just stop on the side of the road somewhere pointed towards 385. Let me get in with you," Chase said.

"Roger that. We'll get to the highway and hold tight. Dark Ford Explorer," August said.

Within minutes Chase saw the SUV parked on the side of the road. Aaron Foster passed it at highway speed, and Chase slowed down and pulled off on the shoulder behind it.

Chase hopped from his truck and ran to the passenger side of the SUV only to find it occupied. Diego was riding shotgun, and Max was sitting behind him. Max opened his door, scooted over behind August, and yelled, "Get in!"

August sped off the second Chase's door was closed. "What are you two doing here?" Chase asked.

"Work trip," Diego said.

"Yeah, glad we didn't miss this," Max said.

Chase filled the group in on his interaction with Aaron Foster as they sped to the intersection of US 385. August slowed enough to allow time for Aaron Foster to make his choice— left to McCamey or right to Fort Stockton.

He turned left and the boys did the same, careful to keep their distance.

"Should we get closer once he's in town? We don't want to lose him," Chase said.

"No, let's accept the chance that we lose sight of him. Mc-Camey is a small enough town to pick him up again if he turns," August said.

US 385 made a ninety-degree left turn in town, and Aaron Foster followed it. He was now headed north towards Crane. He drove out of McCamey for ten miles before his brake lights lit up.

"We got to pass him by," Diego said.

"Yeah, let's make a U-turn and come back. Keep your eyes peeled on what he's doing," August said.

The divided highway took an uncomfortably long time to supply a place to turn around, but August took the first chance he got and gunned it back south on 385.

"He's on Castle Gap Road," Chase said. He was looking at the maps app on his phone. The next gap in the highway median was their turn. "Turn here," Chase said.

August had to slow down if for no reason than to lessen the cloud of dust growing behind them on the oil field road that came off the highway. He did not see a similar cloud coming up in front of them, which made him uncomfortable.

"Where is he?" August asked.

"It looks like this is all oil field roads," Chase said.

"Slow down!" Diego shouted. "He's right up ahead!"

August brought the truck to a crawl on a long curve and then to a stop when Diego signaled with his hand. "That's a gate?" he asked.

Diego had a better view from the passenger side. He said, "Yes, and if we pull up, he'll see us. He's stopped. It's a high fence place. Big gate." The group sat in silence as he relayed Aaron Foster's movements.

"Looks like he's unlocking the gate."

"It's open, he's going to pull through."

"And he's closed it behind him."

Diego signaled to August when it was clear for the group to pull up to the gate. August said, "It has a lockout device on it."

The group got out of the SUV to take a look at the series of padlocks on the gate. "We only need to open one of the padlocks to get in," August said. He pointed to the multi-latch system that allowed multiple parties access to the site without having to share a key or combination.

"These all look locked," Diego said. He pulled on each one individually. Some were keyed and some were combination. "Hold on," he said. "He left one of these unlocked." He removed a padlock from the multi-latch.

Diego opened the gate and stood next to it as the group drove the Explorer through. He then closed it behind them and put the open padlock back in its place.

"I think we can go slow. I only see two ways out of here on the map," Chase said.

August rolled their windows down and drove slowly up the road. Each man was looking out his window for a sign of Aaron Foster. A smaller road would occasionally appear, but each one went only a short distance to an oil field pad site. Each one looked relatively new and active. However, no workers were present.

The road was taking them closer to Castle Gap, which loomed well above them in the distance. The horizon was now dominated by the summits of both King Mountain and Castle Mountain, which sat another 421 feet above the gap itself.

"Slow down, I see him!" Diego said.

August brought the truck to a complete stop, not wanting to risk being spotted. "Is he moving?"

"No, the truck is stopped at the next pad site off to the right. Sit tight. I think I can see it okay from here."

"Diego, stay here with August. Max and I will go up on foot. When you see us near the truck, come up. There's no cell coverage out here for me to call you," Chase said.

Max shot Chase a look that said he didn't appreciate being volunteered for a hike through the prickly brush, but he got out of the truck and quietly closed the door.

"Let's just go take a look," Chase said. They met up in front of the truck, climbed the steep ditch that separated the road from the rugged desert, and headed off through the brush.

19

Broomweed

Max and Chase were moving carefully across the rocky ground, attempting to use the short brush to conceal themselves. Both were scanning the area for signs of Aaron Foster. There was no movement from within the city truck.

As they approached the pad site, it was obvious it was an abandoned oil well. Broomweed was growing sporadically in the once-barren patch cleared for the wellhead. All equipment had been removed, and the city truck was parked on the edge of the site opposite the two men.

As they crouched on the edge of the pad, Chase stood silently and then boldly walked across the rock. Seeing that they had given up concealment, Max also stood and turned towards the Explorer and signaled with his arm for them to approach.

Chase, still scanning the area as he walked, got to the truck first. "It's empty," he mouthed silently to Max, who arrived a second later to confirm.

The two looked around the area until Max tapped on Chase's shoulder and pointed to the edge of the pad, where tire tracks could be seen. They pointed towards the gap itself. Chase silently took off towards them.

Max followed behind and paused to look back at August and Diego. He was able to spot the Ford Explorer moving at not much more than an idle on its way toward them.

Chase guessed they were still almost a mile from the gap itself, and if they were going that far, it would take some time to cross this ground. The tire tracks were faint, but visible enough to follow.

Getting to the gap wasn't a straight climb. There were portions where they'd descend before climbing again. At the top of the crests, Chase would look back at the site and then scan the area ahead for signs of the city manager.

Well over ten minutes into their hike, Max was able to use a high point to wave to August and Diego until they saw him. He wasn't sure if the two would follow them, but at least they'd know where they were headed.

As they reached the next crest, Max dropped to his knees and pulled Chase down with him. He pointed down to the bottom of a deep ravine below them. Chase's eyes followed until he saw a pickup at the lowest point of the draw.

He looked at Max and nodded. "That's Tacy's."

Aaron Foster appeared to have just arrived at the driver's side of the truck. Laying at his feet was a small yellow gas can. He was standing above it as he leaned against the truck, trying to catch his breath. The rise and fall of his chest was visible even from a distance. He held the folder in his other hand.

Time slowed as Max and Chase kneeled, watching Aaron Foster. The man would wipe sweat from his brow but was otherwise motionless, staring blankly into the desert and breathing heavily.

After what felt like several minutes, Aaron Foster straightened himself and opened the driver's side door of the truck. He threw the folder into the vehicle, picked up the yellow canister, unscrewed the top, and threw the open container into the truck. He then reached down and grabbed a red cylinder.

It was a road flare.

Chase sprinted into action. The steep incline propelled him forward, and he struggled to move his feet fast enough to keep upright. He had cut the distance in half before Aaron Foster saw him.

Aaron removed the clear cap from the flare and struck it on the top of the cylinder, causing a fiery spark of molten material to erupt from its end. He turned as Chase reached him and drove the lit flare into Chase's chest.

Chase's momentum drove the pair into the door with brutal force. The smell of burnt flesh filled the air as they crashed to the ground.

A searing pain took over Chase's mind as he lay on his back beside the truck. His ribs felt like they were on fire. He could do nothing more than watch as Aaron Foster rose to his feet above him.

Time had stopped for Chase, trapped by pain. He was relegated to the role of bystander. Aaron Foster was standing over him with a lit road flare, and all Chase wanted to do was sleep. If he just closed his eyes, the pain would go away.

Knowing he had to move to stay alive didn't make his eyelids any lighter. *Get up, Chase! Move!* But he didn't. He couldn't. Even the ear-blistering report of two gunshots didn't fill him with adrenaline.

Foster fell to the ground, crushing Chase beneath him. His weight forced the air out of Chase's lungs. That was enough. Chase's eyes were closing, and there was nothing he could do to prevent it.

But Chase was still aware enough that when Foster fell, the road flare in his hand had fallen into the truck. A wave of fire rushed out of the open door in response. The hot wind brushed across Chase's face and finally triggered an adrenaline response.

Aaron Foster was nothing more than a temporary firewall that protected Chase from the initial blast. Chase rolled the body toward the burning truck—toward the intense and increasing heat—and pushed himself away. He felt someone grab his arms and start dragging him away. It was Max.

Chase's eyes closed, and when he forced them back open, he was sitting upright. It was too bright, but he was face-to-face with Max and Diego.

"He's dead?" Chase asked.

"Yes," Max replied. He had a hand on Chase's shoulder.

"Sorry I missed the fun, but you look a little well-done there, buddy," Diego said. His hand was on Chase's other shoulder. The two were the only thing keeping Chase upright.

"Well-done? Oh . . . overcooked. Funny," Chase said.

Diego continued, "August dropped me off at the truck before going out to find a cell signal so he could call the sheriff. I hope that comes with an ambulance."

"Ambulance? Where's Tacy?" Chase asked.

"No sign of her," Max said.

"You're going to have to walk yourself out of here to get to a hospital," Diego said.

"Hospital? Get the file. We need the file," Chase said, once again frantic to get to the truck.

Max and Diego both stepped aside to give Chase a clear view of the truck that sat roughly a hundred feet away. It was engulfed in flames.

"Did you miss the little bonfire over there?" Max asked.

"No . . . the file is in there," Chase said. It might have been a question.

Aaron Foster's body lay next to the burning truck.

"You shot him?" Chase asked.

"Yes. The flare fell into the truck when I shot him. I think I burned all my hair off just pulling you out of there," Max said, running his hand through his hair.

The conversation was interrupted by August, who called to them from the top of the ridge. Whip was with him. They worked their way down to the trio.

"That was Tacy's car," Chase said. August and Whip both knelt next to Chase to get a better look at him.

"I got that," Whip said. He then stood up. "Here's how this is going to go. August will take Chase up to the trucks. These two stay down here with me. Now hop to it."

Chase's head hurt just as much as his chest. He leaned more heavily on August than he would have liked. The walk back seemed to take forever, but in time they were close enough to see a buzz of activity.

Aaron's city truck, August's SUV, two sheriff department cruisers, and an ambulance were parked with uniformed men moving around the area.

Once they came into clear view of the pad site, two deputies approached them and helped get Chase to the ambulance.

"I'm going to stay up here, if you don't mind. I'll find a cell signal and call Stefan to let him know where they are taking you," August said.

"McCamey," an EMT said.

* * *

By the time Corely and Stefan made it to the hospital, Chase was ready to be discharged. "Burn and a mild concussion. No big deal," he said.

"No big deal . . . that's not what August said," Stefan said.

The three called August from the car. "I just made it home with Max and Diego. All good here," he said. "Whip took our statements. I'm not worried about it."

They kicked around the events of the day before Corely finally asked the question everyone was thinking. "And Tacy?"

"She wasn't in the car. Whip plans to search the area at daybreak," August said.

20

Maximilian's Gold

At 7:53 a.m. the next morning, a member of the search party raised an orange flag above their head and blew a whistle. Chase was there watching from a distance. He was not allowed to take part, and was probably in no condition to anyway. He had needed August to give him a ride, which Whip had requested happen "sooner than later."

Whip was following the line as the search party marched equally spaced apart. They had started at the burned-out truck and were moving towards Castle Gap. This was the first sign of anything. Whip raced over to the raised flag. It wasn't Tacy's body, which Chase was afraid to admit might be resting out here somewhere. Instead, it was a reusable water bottle. Whip raised it above his head.

Many similar stops would occur that morning—a handkerchief, pocketknife, beer and energy drink cans, and too many food wrappers. A surprisingly large number of items for private land in such a remote area, if not for the legend.

J. Frank Dobie's 1930 book, *Coronado's Children*, told the story of the lost gold of Emperor Maximilian I of Mexico. A regular

118

stream of treasure hunters had frequented Castle Gap in search of it ever since. Visitors over the years had failed to make a good impression on the locals. Some went so far as to dynamite the gap looking for the treasure, causing it to be permanently disfigured.

Tacy had told Chase all about this history. She loved it.

Whip headed back up the ravine while his team, having found nothing between the truck and the gap itself, began searching in a different direction. "They'll cover the four points of the compass," Whip told Chase.

Whip took Chase to a sheriff department SUV parked on the oil well pad. They sat in the back seat. "Chase, I appreciate you coming by. How are you feeling?" he asked.

"Fine. Doc said to take it easy for a day or two. How's the search?"

"They haven't found anything, but they're still looking. I wanted to get your statement as soon as possible, and I assumed you'd prefer me to do it rather than a state trooper."

"The state is coming in?"

"A city official was killed, so that's sort of an automatic thing. It will be a Texas Ranger, actually, and you might still need to talk to them. At least I can have a complete set of interviews for them when they get here."

"I guess you saw that you've got camera crews in town."

"Yes, and they can stay there all they want. I don't need the press. I got volunteers from three counties out here this morning without their help."

Once the two got down to business, Chase answered the sheriff's questions honestly. Well, he did leave out the part about breaking into Tacy's house. Otherwise, he told him everything he knew plus when and how he knew it. None of it seemed to be news to Whip.

The focus of the conversation was the day of the shooting, mostly the events immediately before and after Aaron lit the road flare.

"There was accelerant in the Jeep . . . diesel most likely," Whip said.

They went over the shooting itself and then Aaron Foster's files. "You haven't seen them?" Chase asked.

"That's not a priority, but we did lay eyes on his office."

"And you saw the files?"

"You tell me. What did he show you?"

It was repetitive. Chase recounted his time in Aaron Foster's office forwards and backwards.

"Why didn't you call 9-1-1?"

"I assumed that keeping a file about Tacy wasn't illegal."

"But it was urgent enough for you to trespass onto private property and confront him?"

"The gate was unlocked. I believe that August did call you as soon as we had cell reception."

Whip had Chase repeat everything again and again.

"Tacy's truck. That's what got me to act. That's what made it urgent," Chase said.

"And why do you think he led you right to Tacy's vehicle?"

"I think I spooked him. I got too close."

"Too close to what?"

"I don't know. He didn't wander out here on accident. Something happened to Tacy. Something bad. And he had something to do with it. That folder might have been the only thing that explained what happened."

Whip finally seemed content that he had what he needed. "Okay. Best if you get out of here."

Chase opened the door and started to get out but instead turned back to Whip. "Was there a folder on Foster's desk? I wrote 'Airport Research' on it."

"I don't know. Is it important?"

"Yes, Turner Cam and Aaron Foster both thought that was all of Tacy's research into the airport."

"The whistleblowing stuff? What you said caused Turner Cam to lose his mind?"

"Yes. I left it on his desk. It was on that desk when Aaron and I left city hall yesterday."

"What was in it?" Whip asked.

"Financials and contracts I printed off the city's website. Junk principally. Filler. Nonsense. A few of the pages are Tacy's real notes. I put just enough in there to send someone on a wild goose chase and waste a bunch of time."

"I'll have someone look."

21

Bon Camarade

Chase was sitting in his apartment having just finished his new morning routine of staying inside and avoiding the press. The need to find a "real job" was weighing on him. The weight had increased each day since the shooting. He couldn't work because of the fog in his head and the pain in his ribs. It also didn't help that he had been named in an active Texas Rangers investigation.

Chase had taken his search for Tacy digital and spent his days searching social media and calling dead end after dead end. Max had his own problems, and Diego and August had their hands busy with some state contract.

In addition to spinning his wheels online, Chase had filed numerous open records requests with the city. The city treated his requests like a game. They'd say that the state law didn't define "prompt" or "reasonable," which was all the Public Records Act said about how quickly to respond to a request. Each time he got someone to answer the phone, they'd make it sound like his requests were unreasonable and needed more time to complete.

He asked for everything on the city truck that burned, emails and records about Tacy, and numerous records surrounding the airport. He had spent his morning starting a complaint with the Texas Attorney General hoping that might get him some answers.

Chase's typing was interrupted by the buzzing of his phone. He grabbed the keys to his truck after reading the message. Within twenty minutes he'd be at August's ranch. Instead of pulling up in front of the main house, he stopped on the property at a much more modest hunting lodge.

As Chase closed the door of his truck, the front door of the lodge opened and closed. There stood Max on the front porch. For the first time since the incident, he looked happy.

"What's up?" Chase asked.

"My lawyer doesn't think they are going to prosecute. They said it was a clean shoot," Max said. A broad smile broke out across his face.

Chase gave him a hug as the front door opened again and out stepped Max's wife, Sarah. Chase released one arm from around Max to draw her into a three-person hug.

"Group hug," she said. They all laughed.

"I know you're relieved," Chase said.

"All good. All good," she said. They broke from the embrace.

"Yeah, we're thinking about making this move permanent . . ." Max said. He swept his arm out as if to present the hunting cabin to Chase. "But obviously not this specific place."

"We can't go back to Houston. Our friends and neighbors stopped returning our calls the second Max was in the news. Plus, neither one of our girls decided to go back to Houston after college. They can come to visit us here just as easily as anywhere," Sarah said.

"Our girls don't worry about anything," Max said.

"They called Max a hero the minute we told them what happened," Sarah added.

"Well, Max did save my life. He is a hero, a *bon camarade*," Chase said.

"Enough of that. We wanted to tell you first, but August is waiting for us up at the house. We're going to celebrate," Max said.

At the house, the group was quickly joined by both Beldames. Corely barely broke stride as she entered the house and dropped a folder of documents on the counter in front of Chase. "A new clue," she said. She stared at the folder waiting for him to open it.

The first document was a map from the county appraisal district website. It showed the land bordering the city airport and listed who owned it. All of it was a large ranch owned by Baxter Whitey.

"Baxter owns a lot of land," Chase noted.

"Yes, I printed that out for you because the next document will make a lot more sense once you understand that he has a ranch that surrounds the airport on all sides."

While reading the second document, Chase asked, "Gary and Ward?"

"Those are two other counties with similar airports that were expanded by a company called Scout Commercial Partners," she explained.

"Who is that?"

"Real estate investors that specialize in rural airports."

"They weren't mentioned in the pitch to the EDC."

"No, but Diego decided to take a look at takeoffs and landings at the airport. There's a free website that tracks all that. He bounced a few names off of us, all locals. The only outlier was Scout Commercial Partners. A Google search returned their rural airport projects."

"What do they have to do with Baxter owning the surrounding land?"

"My guess is the city can't afford to buy the land from Baxter, so these guys are in the deal to solve that. They did that for these other two projects as well."

As the others assembled in August's front room, each took their turn reading the documents and offering their thoughts.

"Do we know when this meeting happened?" August asked.

"We know when the flight happened. It was right after Tacy was fired and rehired," Corely said.

"That week? So this is the meeting Tacy said she was left out of?" Chase asked.

"We think so," Corely replied.

22

Summoned

Turner Cam didn't bother to get up. In fact, he didn't even bother to look up from his computer, even when he spoke. "You can't help but step on a few toes when you insist on running around in the dark . . . and you've stepped on plenty."

Chase couldn't help but think that summoning someone to his office must be a regular thing for the mayor. Apparently it was now Chase's turn.

"I'm a fighter. I fight for this community. You know I used to box in college?" Turner asked Chase, who still stood just inside the office door.

"I did not," Chase replied. He took a seat in one of the two chairs that sat on the other side of Turner's leather-top desk. He was relishing the moment he could tell Stefan about this conversation.

"So, if you'd like to take this outside. This time I won't have my back turned."

"I'm sure that won't be necessary." This would get some good laughs at the Butterfield.

"You called Scout Commercial Partners, I'm told." Turner

leaned back in a red leather office chair. "Why did you choose to do that?"

"The guys that want Baxter Whitey's land to expand the airport?" Chase asked. He couldn't fully contain the smile attempting to break free across his lips.

Turner furrowed his brow. "No, the guys that wanted to invest in our community. That may never happen because of you and your buddies. They were spooked by your incident with Aaron Foster."

"My incident?" Chase thought before replying. "I heard they flew to town to look at the airport. It sounds like they want to make a big investment."

"Wanted. Past tense, if you keep things up. That's revenue lost because of you and Max. We might as well throw Stefan in there too."

Turner leaned forward and resumed typing on the computer perched on the edge of his desk.

"It was tail numbers," Chase said. "I looked at all the flights that came to the airport, and a few stood out, like Scout Commercial Partners. Those flights are reported on free flight tracking websites, and a little Google search was all I needed to see that they do some big aviation projects—especially at rural municipal airports."

Turner didn't bother to look up from his typing. "Why were you looking at tail numbers?"

"Not important," Chase said. That got Turner to look up from his keyboard. Chase continued, "Their plane landed here during the week that Tacy was rehired by the EDC. When she told everyone that the city had stopped including her in meetings, this is the meeting she meant. That was a threat," Chase said.

"I brought you here to make a choice," Turner said. He set a large folder on his desk. The folder of fake leads Chase left on Aaron Foster's desk.

"I bet the sheriff is looking for that," Chase said. "He'd probably like to know how it got from Aaron Foster's desk to yours."

"This is bunk. You're going to give me her real files, drop your open records requests, never contact Scout Commercial Partners again, and keep your nose out of this deal."

"Or what?"

"Your little assault charge comes back. Aggravated assault is what I'm told they call it. A felony. Ten years in big boy prison."

Chase stood and began walking to the door when he stopped. He spoke over his shoulder. "What do they call this?" He turned towards Turner. "I don't mean this little conversation. I mean the airport deal. Crony capitalism? Everybody gets a big payday, and the taxpayer is left with the bill? Were you going to get a nice payday?"

Turner didn't respond.

"If you put half the energy into streets and water as you do that airport, we'd be on our way to fixing this place," Chase said.

"Max killed Aaron Foster. You, Max, and Stefan are destroying this town," Turner said. He began moving around the edge of his desk.

Chase continued facing Turner while reaching a hand behind him, searching for the doorknob. "You'll end up in the same place as Aaron Foster. Cremated. Some private, out-of-town service. No press. No friends. Not even an obituary in the newspaper."

Turner closed the distance between them faster than Chase

could have predicted. There was no sign of a limp. Before Chase could react, he was eating a straight right punch. Chase staggered back against the door and brought both hands up defensively. He could feel the blood run from his nose and tasted it run over his lips. *He really did box in college*, he thought.

Turner had wound up for another right to Chase's head, but Chase was able to easily block it, leaving an opening for Chase to bend down and drive his shoulder into Turner's waist. At the same time, he wrapped both arms around Turner's legs and drew his knees towards him. A classic double-leg takedown from his wrestling days.

His legs gone from under him, Turner fell backwards onto the hardwood floor. He landed with a sickening thud, like a watermelon falling on concrete. Chase scrambled to his feet and then noticed Turner wasn't moving. There was no blood, but he was unconscious.

Chase felt for a pulse in Turner's neck. His own pulse was sky-high. He was a purser not a medic, but he was able to catch a steady rise and fall from Turner's chest. *Good, he's alive*, Chase thought.

Chase rolled Turner onto his side, bent his leg to keep him from rolling over, and tilted his head back slightly.

He then stood and walked behind Turner Cam's desk while dialing 9-1-1 on his phone. He sat in Turner's chair, brought his shoulder up to trap his phone against his ear, and began typing on Turner's computer.

His call was immediately answered. Chase asked for police and medical. He said he had been attacked by the mayor. He gave them the address to Turner's private office and said that the assailant—that's what he called him—was breathing and that Chase had placed him in the safety position. The 9-1-1 operator clarified that he meant the first aid recovery position that best kept an unconscious person's airway open.

Chase continued to type and move the mouse as he spoke. The operator continued to ask Chase questions. He provided his name and phone number. He answered questions about Turner as best he could. He guessed at his age, but didn't know if he had any medical conditions or took any medication.

Chase continued typing even as the operator walked him through checking for a pulse. He never left the keyboard, but did respond positively while he kept an eye on the door and an eye on Turner.

The sound of a siren in the distance was eventually followed by the turning of the doorknob.

The first person through the door was a deputy, who found Chase kneeling next to Turner. Chase provided no statement, and this time he meant it.

23

Balsamic Beef

Chase was searing a roast in a large pan in his kitchen. He was making a heck of a mess. Butter was popping all over the stove as he relayed to Stefan that he had been released from his interview with the sheriff's deputy without any charges . . . yet. His lawyer made it clear that he could expect a warrant to be issued at any time.

Stefan broke the silence. "We're just going to sit here and cook dinner like everything is okay?"

"Everything is absolutely not okay. Do you know the only people that ask me about Tacy?" Chase didn't wait for an answer. "Folks down at the church, you and Corely, and August and Max. That's it. The rest of this town acts like her truck being burned is just some sort of crazy coincidence. Like Aaron Foster just took a wrong turn with a road flare in his hand."

He sprinkled a dry seasoning on the roast and then turned it using large metal tongs. "Oh, and a Class C misdemeanor is nothing to sneeze at, and a third-degree felony carries up to ten years in jail. I could get one of each, or maybe two of the big one. Even if I don't, the lawyer is going to bankrupt me."

"I'm not sure that's the case. The whole town thinks—" Stefan stopped himself.

"Thinks what?"

"They think . . . you know."

"Think what?"

"Aaron Foster killed Tacy."

"I think we all know that Aaron Foster killed Tacy, Stefan," Chase said. He had never said it out loud. It hit him like a ton of bricks. He fell back and caught himself on the countertop. It took all he had not to cry in front of Stefan.

Stefan raced over and turned the stove off. He moved the pan off the burner and started wiping up the splattered grease. He didn't look at Chase.

"Hey, uh, what's the next step?" Stefan asked. "Never mind, I can follow this recipe."

Stefan moved the roast to the slow cooker. He added the balsamic vinegar, olive oil, and beef broth that were sitting on the counter already. He turned the device on and closed the lid.

"Hey." He still had his back to Chase. "I got a call today."

Chase took a deep breath. "From who?"

"Baxter Whitey, by way of an intermediary. You are being offered a 'clean slate.' You won't have to worry about any charges. Turner Cam is awake and doing fine. Baxter would even like you to be the one that tells the story to the newspaper."

"I bet he wouldn't."

"This is a serious offer. You tell the paper you went over there to talk about the project and found Turner Cam in his office unconscious. He fell off a ladder changing a light bulb or something."

"Changing a light bulb? That's the dumbest idea I've ever heard."

"This is a legitimate offer."

"Why would Turner go along with this?"

"Well . . . you are going to help correct the record on this airport project. Say there have been misunderstandings and that it's worth a fresh look," Stefan said.

"That's it?"

"They said you knew the rest of the deal. Whatever Turner told you. What did he tell you?"

"To turn over Tacy's research and then drop it. The open records requests, everything."

"I'm not telling you to do that. I'm not sure what you should do, but you had to know this was an offer."

"How do you make this happen?"

"A game of telephone. I call someone, they call someone else, the newspaper lady comes over, you tell your story, and then everything goes away."

"Do it."

* * *

Chase had never met Rebecca Whitey, but there she sat. The smell of balsamic beef had only just begun to fill the room from the slow cooker that ticked away time on the kitchen countertop. Stefan was the one that answered the door and invited her in. She walked in already explaining the need to get an article done before the printer produced that week's edition.

"What prompted you to go to Turner Cam's office?" she asked. She sat in the swivel chair he used for his desk in his wide-open apartment.

"We were going to chat about this big airport project," Chase replied. He pulled out a chair from his dining table, a comfortable distance from her, but close enough to speak easily. He turned it toward her and sat down.

Stefan leaned against the kitchen counter some feet away.

"You went there to clear the air?" Rebecca asked.

"Clean slate, I think you call it," Chase said.

"So, you went to his office, and that's when you found him unconscious?"

"No," Chase said. He paused briefly but saw no reaction. "He was very much conscious when I saw him." A sly smile spread across his lips. He couldn't help it.

Rebecca's eyebrows shot up momentarily. Stefan chuckled lightly, which earned him a stern look from Rebecca. Chase looked at him to confirm he was enjoying the unexpected twist.

Rebecca regained her poker face. "Then what happened?"

"He showed me a file that he stole from Aaron's office that detailed all the problems at the airport. He thought it was a copy of all of Tacy Vernon's research, but it was rubbish. I planted it there. You know all of this."

"I do?" She sat straight up in her chair as if ready to take notes for a routine story.

"He also showed me a copy of the notes from the meeting between Scout Commercial Partners, Turner Cam, Aaron Foster, and your husband."

"And I know this how?"

"Aaron Foster sure does like to leave a paper trail."

Rebecca stood.

Chase stood as well. "Turner showed me Aaron's notes. They were right there on his computer. He turned on you. He gave them to me. He wants a way out of this."

"No."

"Scout Commercial Partners laid out all of their demands.

They will help the city secure federal and state grants, which they get a cut of during construction. Then a big grant from the local EDC, which has to be borrowed, plus tax breaks on whatever is built. In exchange, they buy your husband's land for a big premium."

"No."

"You and Baxter only get big money for your land if the city rolls out the red carpet. You have to make sure the local politicians remain compliant. The Whiteys win again at the game of corporate welfare."

Rebecca stood stone-faced as Chase continued.

"I then asked him about Tacy Vernon. He lost it. He punched me in the face, and I defended myself. You can print that."

Rebecca looked to Stefan and then back to Chase. She did not speak.

Chase continued as he stood over his chair. "That's not all Turner said. Poor Aaron Foster. How deep in his head did you folks get?"

"No, whatever that stupid man did has nothing to do with me," Rebecca said.

"Things got out of hand. Tacy was going to blow it all up. What did you do to stop her?"

"Nothing." She turned to the door. "Nothing at all," she said as she walked out of the door.

Chase sat back down in his chair with a loud exhale.

Stefan grabbed one of the many bottles that lined the backsplash of Chase's kitchen countertop. He collected two glasses from a cabinet and sat at the table next to Chase. "How much of what you said is true?"

"Probably all of it."

"Even the stuff about the mayor?"

"Oh, I embellished the facts a bit there. I searched his computer and found a copy of Aaron Foster's notes from the meeting with Scout Commercial Partners. Turner Cam will be surprised to find out that he turned on Baxter Whitey."

The two took a sip of their whiskey.

"Who called you to set up this deal tonight?" Chase asked.

"A fellow—well, former—EDC board member. Brady Laye."

24

Folder

Chase returned to the Butterfield the next morning. He expected to see a deputy sheriff at any moment, but the day passed without being arrested. He took control of what little he could—his morning routine. He finished his complaint to the Texas Attorney General, which he hoped would get him some clues.

Another day later and that routine would finally bring him face-to-face with whatever Rebecca Whitey decided to write about him. He ignored the fresh newspaper on the table until he had his Americano. Sitting down in his usual leather chair, he expected the front page to be dedicated to him. "Villain of the Year" or "Man Attacks Mayor" would be about right. Perhaps Rebecca Whitey would use the paper to bury the mayor. "Mayor Steals File in Missing Woman's Case," but only if she believed the lie that the mayor had turned on her and Baxter.

Instead, the front page was another puff piece on the airport project.

"EDC to Pave Way for New Airport Jobs"

Chase was tempted to skip it, as it appeared to be the same old propaganda. However, it did mention that the EDC would be revisiting the loan at their next meeting, that night. Chase knew they had the votes to pass it, but he planned to attend the meeting anyway.

Deeper into the paper was a lone paragraph on the mayor:

Mayor Turner Cam, who suffered a medical episode at a recent public meeting, was found unconscious in his office. It is unclear whether the events are linked. He is expected to make a full recovery and hopes to return to work soon. He thanks the public for the outpouring of support.

What a joke.

Chase also saw an advertisement for a job opening. The EDC was looking for a new director.

* * *

"I didn't sign up for this," Brady said. He was standing in front of the counter at Laye Texas Meats. "It's done. I'm done. Accept it and move on."

Chase couldn't argue with Brady's frustration. The man had probably thought serving on the board of the EDC would be a simple way to give back to the community. Instead, he got threatened by the mayor and then Baxter Whitey pressured him to resign.

However, he had got Stefan to set up the meeting between Chase and Rebecca. He needed to explain that.

"How'd you find yourself setting up a meeting between me and the newspaper lady?"

"I don't know anything about that." Brady began putting fresh steaks into a refrigerated display case.

"I know you were involved."

"I know you don't know how serious all of this is. That's

what I know."

"Serious enough to kill? What do you think happened to Tacy?"

"A hundred years ago they had a reliable way to solve a problem around here. They'd fill your boots up," Brady said. "They'd drown their problems in the Pecos, and if there was anything left, the wild animals would clean it up."

"Aaron Foster and Turner Cam did that to Tacy?"

"Well, the mayor has the temper for it. He wasn't the one shot burning her truck, though."

"Was Baxter Whitey involved?"

"Nope. You think he's killing anyone over an airport? You just see up close how these families run the town. You think that a bunch of good old boys run everything? They do, and some of them are not good people, and they hold a grudge for life. Congrats. You figured it out," Brady said.

"And the money? Tacy uncovered a lot of questionable stuff at the airport."

"Has it ever occurred to you that the city manager was simply bad at his job? He was just the next man up over at the city when the last manager left. The mayor is a jerk, the city manager was incompetent, and one powerful family didn't like not getting their way," Brady said. "Plus, the deal is done. The city council voted to give the mayor the authority to negotiate and sign the deal."

"When did they do this?"

"Maybe two or three years ago. The city council voted to delegate everything to the mayor. That turned the whole project into a black box. None of us would have even known about the details if they didn't need money from the EDC. Tonight they'll get their money, and we'll all go back to not knowing what's going on."

"I didn't realize the project was that old."

"No one was really paying attention. I'm not sure anyone even looked at it with a critical eye until the EDC tabled that vote. It isn't anything more than what it looks like. The city manager delivered Baxter a payday. And this isn't about the airport anymore anyway. This is about telling those people no. That isn't tolerated," Brady said.

* * *

Chase had a beer at the Butterfield before the EDC meeting. It did little to soothe his frustrations, but he had a second one anyway. Once it was time, he walked over to the Chamber of Commerce. He was early enough to have to ask for the sign-in sheet. One of the board members handed him a blank sheet of paper. He would be the first one to speak that night.

The room filled up fast, and almost everyone signed the sheet to speak at the start of the meeting. He knew about half of the room, all members of St. Stephen.

When the meeting started, the chairman explained the public comment period. Everyone who signed up could speak for three minutes. Instead of going off the list, he simply looked at the crowd and asked who would be first.

"Me," Chase said. He stood as more than one audible groan left the crowd. He assumed that the pro-airport crowd had planned to speak first. Perhaps the chairman had even purposefully ignored the order of names on the list so they could. But Chase had beat them to it.

There was no podium or microphone. Chase simply stood at the front of the room and looked at the board. "When this project was first pitched in this very room, it was voted down. It was voted down because it loses money."

Murmurs could be heard from some in the crowd.

"In response, our city leaders, many of you all here right now, turned a blind eye to the retaliatory firing of the EDC director. You did the same when board members were forced to resign because they refused to vote your way."

Most of the board never made eye contact with Chase. They instead focused on the single-page agenda in their hands.

"It has since been discovered that accounting errors are the norm over at the airport. EDC funds may or may not be used to cover up these problems. At no point have you disclosed your connections to Baxter Whitey or the potential conflicts of interest as he profits from the project."

Many of the board members shook their heads.

"And Tacy." He paused to collect himself. "Tacy Vernon." He took a deep breath. "Well, our elected officials have stolen, destroyed, or buried files that might explain her disappearance."

"No," someone from the crowd said. Chase turned, but not to look at them. He looked at the door and walked towards it. The crossed arms and stern faces of half the audience was enough.

The door chimed as it opened, he stepped through, and let it clang shut loudly behind him. Chase was settling back into a barstool at the Butterfield as Hayden approached his end of the bar.

"How was it?" Hayden asked.

"I said my piece and left. They are going to vote however they vote."

It was at most two hours before Stefan and Corely arrived and took seats next to Chase. By then, he had finished dinner and put away another few drinks.

Stefan slid a stapled trio of pages over to him. "Their brochure," he said.

"What happened after I left?" Chase asked as he thumbed through the papers.

"We had over an hour of public comments. About half the room echoed what you said."

"And the other half?"

"Basically a Whitey Family Holdings company meeting. Their employees, family, and friends did everything but call you a liar by name," Corely added.

"Was Baxter there?"

"Nope," Stefan said.

"After the comments, a guy from Scout Commercial Partners presented that brochure. Scout expands the airport and the city gets more 'nights in hotels' and 'meals at restaurants' from visiting pilots. He repeated the same 'hundreds of thousands of dollars' claim Aaron Foster used when he pitched the economic benefits of an expanded airport," Corely said.

"The board ate it up. Passed the thing unanimously," Stefan said.

"How could Tacy have found out about Scout?" Chase asked.

"I don't know," Corely replied.

"Let's go find out."

* * *

While they were driving to Tacy's, Chase said, "There's a folder at Tacy's for SCP. I thought it was just receipts. Shield Cooperative Protection, the big insurance company."

"So what? How many brokers are in a town this small? SCP probably covers half of us," Stefan said.

"What if SCP is Scout Commercial Partners?" Chase asked.

He pulled into Tacy's driveway and stopped alongside her house.

"Hold on! Isn't this an active crime scene or something?" Corely asked. Chase was already out the door and to the bathroom window. He pushed it open and slipped inside.

He poked his head out, saw the two still sitting in his idling truck staring back at him, and closed the window.

As soon as Chase took a step back, he stepped on something. He spun around and saw that Tacy's cabinets were open with several things spilled on the floor. He turned on the screen of his phone and entered the hallway. Her bedroom was the same. The dresser drawers and her closet were open, and clothes were thrown around.

Her entire unit was a mess. The small living room was the exception. Any papers Chase had left on the small table were gone. The little shelf above her desk where her folders had been neatly aligned was empty.

Someone had ransacked her duplex, and the SCP folder was gone.

25

Drafted

"Chase, what's the latest with your open records requests?" August asked loud enough to catch the attention of everyone assembled at the weekly breakfast at St. Stephen.

"What open records requests?" Hayden asked. Clearly not everyone was up to speed on Chase's issues with the city.

"The night Tacy went missing, a city truck caught fire," Chase explained.

August added, "It happened to be driven by our mayor and, may he rest in peace, the former city manager."

"Yes," Chase said. "Requests for any details on that, any records they have on Tacy, and information about the airport project have all been ignored by the city. They've used every trick: Claimed my requests are too broad, that providing the information is too 'burdensome'—"

"Doing their jobs seems too burdensome most of the time," a church regular joked.

"Right!" Chase replied. "I finally asked the Texas Attorney General to help."

"What came of that?" August asked.

"Nothing yet. It's frustrating."

"I did an open records request of my own. Either they don't know me down there, or they didn't think what I requested would be a problem," August said.

"What did you request?" Hayden asked.

"Just a copy of Turner Cam's application to appear on the ballot as he seeks his fourth term as mayor."

"Over my dead body," Chase said.

"I figured you'd feel that way. The city staff has a history of throwing out applications like this. They conveniently wait until the deadline to run for office and then magically find an issue with the paperwork. The mayor has run the last two times unopposed with this little trick," August said.

A few of the old-timers nodded in agreement.

August continued, "My guess is that if you copy his application, your campaign for mayor will start without any problems." He looked at Chase.

"My campaign for mayor?" Chase asked.

"Yep, congrats! I got your application all filled out. I'll be your treasurer—if you don't mind—and we can swing by city hall today to file it before the deadline."

"All in favor?" Hayden asked as he raised his hand.

It looked to Chase as if every hand went up.

"Great, the first very unofficial action of our breakfast club has passed!" Hayden joked.

The breakfast devolved into individual conversations as the plates of food were passed around. At last, the meal ended with the usual assignment of tasks for the next week.

As Chase got up to leave, trailed by August, he found himself face-to-face with Whip.

"Did you hire a PI to look into Tacy Vernon's disappearance?"

Whip asked.

Chase guessed the sheriff already knew the answer.

"Actually, it was me. I didn't hire anyone. I've been doing it all myself."

"Somebody might ask why a candidate for mayor would decide to cowboy around a missing person's case. They might say it shows bad judgment to not have reported her missing sooner. Your two run-ins with the mayor don't show the best judgment either. Lucky for you, bad judgment seems to be your opponent's specialty. I doubt you could beat him at his own game of very public and very poor decisions."

"I hear you," Chase said. "Any sign of her phone or laptop?"

"All I can say is we're looking for her."

"What about the Texas Rangers?"

"If I could share any details with you, I want you to under-stand I would."

"And I trust you never found that file I told you was left on Aaron Foster's desk."

"Actually, no, we didn't."

"That's a detail."

"I'm a better friend than enemy. You could be behind bars right now." Whip turned and began shaking hands and exchanging goodbyes on his way to the door.

Chase caught up with him again outside. "I have a detail for you," he said.

"Alright."

"The mayor has that file. It was on his desk when he . . . was allegedly found unconscious."

"That's a surprise, but not surprising, if that makes sense. It is possible, let's say, that Tacy's cell phone was in her truck. If it was, it went straight to Castle Gap from the city council meeting and never left. Remnants of it and her laptop were in her truck."

"Okay. Let's say, hypothetically, that someone went by Tacy's duplex and saw that her files were all gone and her place was a mess—thoroughly searched. That would be something to look into."

"Probably, yes."

"Thank you."

* * *

August and Chase parked against the curb out front. The building looked empty as they pushed the swinging commercial door open and stepped inside. Not a single employee in sight. City hall was a wide-open building that better resembled a bank. In fact, the city employees worked behind teller windows that surrounded the open center of the room.

On the drive over, August had given Chase a warning about the staff that he had learned from their handling of his own open records request. It wasn't as trouble-free as he'd originally let on. "At first, they claimed they didn't know where the open records request form was. Then, they refused to take the request because the lady that accepts them wasn't in the office," August said.

The teller windows that surrounded the open center of the room were full of glare where the mid-morning sun bounced off the polished floor and reflected off the glass. Finally, an unwelcoming female voice came from somewhere behind the wall of glass. "May I help you?"

"Sure, I have a form to submit. Where do you want it?" Chase asked. He squinted and tried to figure out where the voice was coming from.

"You can bring it over here," she said. This did nothing to help him find her. He decided to just walk in the general direction of her voice and set his paperwork on the counter closest to where he guessed she was located. He was one window off.

Once he almost had his nose pressed against the glass window, he could finally see a figure behind the next window to his left. He shifted over and handed her his paperwork through the small rectangular hole between the glass and the countertop.

The woman looked at the document but made no effort to pick it up. "I can't take this. It must go to the city secretary, and she isn't in."

"You're telling me that I can't submit this official application to a city employee at city hall during regular business hours?" he asked. He knew this would not help improve her attitude.

"You can leave it there and maybe she'll see it, or you can come back."

"I need you to take this and give me a receipt." He was confident he was just making this worse, but it wasn't just that he didn't want to repeat this later. What if the city secretary stayed gone all day? He'd miss the deadline.

To his surprise, the woman's hand came up and snatched the document aggressively. She then wrote out a makeshift receipt on a pre-printed pad meant to record missed phone calls. She handed it to him.

"Good enough for me! Thank you!" he said.

She didn't respond.

Chase was running for mayor.

26

Polish Parliament

"You know I used to box in college?" The bar erupted in laughter.

That was the scene Chase walked into that evening. Stefan was holding court with Hayden, Max, and several locals.

"And there he is," Stefan said. The small crowd turned to Chase.

"Mr. Mayor," Hayden said.

"We'll see," Chase replied with a laugh. A beer had already been poured for him by the time he made it to the bar.

The group joked about Chase's latest run-in with the mayor. They moved on to other topics before the night was cut short by an event at the high school. Stefan suggested they go up to Chase's place instead of sitting at an empty bar.

"Good idea," Chase said.

There really wasn't a faster way to Chase's place than walking to the end of the block and going back up the alley to the stairs.

The three walked around the corner of the building and turned into the alley. Chase stopped first, and the others quickly followed. From this distance in the dark, it looked like the door to his apartment was wide open.

It was!

He sprinted to the bottom of the stairs. Max followed close behind and drew his Glock G43X pistol. They took the steps two at a time, Stefan trailing behind. The sound of their feet landing heavily on the steps echoed through the alley. Halfway up, Max drew a small flashlight from his pocket, turned it on, and pressed it back against his other hand to brace the pistol.

The light bobbed around wildly as Max took each step.

When they reached the top of the stairs, Max took the lead into the unlit, pitch-black apartment.

All the flashlights in the world would not have helped his brain better understand the chaotic scene. A second or two after entering, Chase flipped the light switch by the door.

The entire apartment, which was really just one large room, had clearly been searched by someone who wasn't concerned about leaving a trail.

The papers from Chase's desk were scattered across the room. Was it careless or purposeful? Someone had not only searched his desk, but seemed to have left as big a mess as they could.

Every drawer and cabinet had been left open, but the contents were still inside.

"What in the world?" Stefan asked. He had finally made it up the stairs.

Max made his way, gun still drawn, to the only door in the place—the bathroom. He confirmed it was clear and returned the Glock to his waistband holster under his untucked shirt.

Chase and Stefan walked around the room surveying the mess.

"What do you think they wanted?" Stefan asked.

"Tacy's files."

"Doesn't August have those?" Max asked from across the room.

"The originals, yes, but I have a copy. Plus a load of notes," Chase replied.

The three picked up papers and called out what they were as they went.

"Bills."

"Gun records."

"Receipts."

This continued until everything was sorted on his dining table. It would take some time to reorder the paperwork from his gun business, but otherwise it was obvious what was missing.

"All of Tacy's stuff is gone. I think that's it," Chase said.

"Do we call the sheriff?" Stefan asked.

Max looked to Chase. The two hesitated to answer.

"Have to," Chase finally said. He walked over to the whiskey bottles that lined his kitchen backsplash.

"What do we win by doing that?" Max asked.

"Nothing good, probably."

* * *

Max, Stefan, and Chase were sitting around the table drinking whiskey when Whip walked in. Every drawer and cabinet in the apartment was still open.

"What have you boys gotten yourselves into?" Whip asked.

"Polish Parliament," Stefan said.

"What?"

"A big mess."

"Somebody went through the place, scattered these files from wall to wall"—Chase waved his arm over the stacks of papers on the table—"and stole all of Tacy's research into the airport."

"And you fellas decided to sit here and have a drink?"

"Well, I poured the drinks, confirmed my gun inventory is still here, and then tried to catch up with these two," Chase said.

"They didn't mess with your gun safe?" Whip asked.

"No, and they didn't dump the drawers or cabinets on the floor. My guess is they found what they were looking for, or they didn't want to make too much noise with us downstairs at the bar," Chase said.

"You know we have to inform the ATF?" Whip asked.

"Yes."

"This will just be a box-checking exercise then," Whip said.

"No worries. Speaking of, what did you find at Tacy's?"

"It got the Russian Parliament treatment too."

"Polish," Stefan chimed in.

"Sure, okay. The Texas Rangers are on it."

"And the fake files the mayor stole?"

"The security cameras in city hall just happen to be on the fritz. There's no recording of your run-in with Aaron Foster or anything that happened in his office after."

"Convenient," Max said.

"Very," Chase added.

27

Twenty Citations

After the next St. Stephen breakfast, Chase spent a full day putting up campaign signs. Lots of people were giving him advice, including August, who had ordered signs for him within hours of filing his application at city hall. Once they arrived, Chase spent his mornings putting them up around town.

It felt like he was putting up a fence each time he erected the almost comically large yard signs. It was amazing how fast word spread although it was only within the congregation of St. Stephen. He was getting calls, texts, and emails every day asking for a sign.

The mayor wasn't putting any signs out, or at least his campaign wasn't doing so yet. Chase was told he might be the first local candidate to ever put so many out.

When Chase turned out of the church parking lot after the next weekly breakfast, he wasn't greeted by the sight of the two signs he had put up on that block just days before.

He turned again towards another cluster of three signs he had put up nearby. Those were gone too.

Chase pulled the truck over to open his phone and try to find an AirTag location. That was another one of August's ideas. There was an AirTag Bluetooth tracker in each of the signs. They were small enough to go unnoticed.

Once he opened the app, he was greeted by a surprising sight. All of his AirTags were in the same place! As he zoomed in on the map it became clear that every tag was sitting inside one building—city hall.

Chase pointed his truck in that direction singularly focused on finding those signs. As he opened the door to the building, he was met by a familiar face. The woman who had taken his application to run for mayor was sitting behind the glass, the only visible occupant in the building. His signs were nowhere in sight.

"Do you have my yard signs?" he asked as he approached the glass.

"Mr. Haven. Yes, we do. You must speak to the city inspector. He's not in, though," she said. She looked for, and found, a business card that she slid over to Chase. "You'll need to call him to discuss the violations."

Violations? Chase robbed her of the opportunity for an argument. In fact, he didn't offer her a response at all. He was already punching the phone number into his phone as he walked out of city hall. His call was answered before he reached his truck.

"Yes, sir. Your signs are in violation of state law. There's no warning printed on them advising that they can't be put within the highway right-of-way. Every political sign in the state must include the disclaimer."

"Okay."

"You can pay us to destroy the signs, or you can pick them up and destroy them yourself."

I'm not destroying anything, was Chase's first thought, but he stopped himself. He agreed to retrieve his signs and remained polite. By noon that day Chase had his signs and he was putting them back up, complete with newly printed stickers containing the required disclosure.

* * *

That night's city council meeting, the last one before the election, was lightly attended and featured a short, routine agenda. The council progressed through the normal consent agenda, approval of minutes, and regular city reports only after a small delay getting started. Mayor Turner Cam was not in attendance, and that appeared to Chase to have been an unexpected event. Why else would they all look around the table at each other waiting for him to appear?

The city secretary, who appeared to be acting as the interim city manager, presented her report. She walked the council through a "housekeeping item" involving the airport budget.

"Our treasurer needs to restate some previous financial reports. We've changed how we account for certain expenses, corrected some minor errors, and recategorized some items," she explained.

One of the council members that had given Tacy a hard time chimed in to reassure the council that this was just a "housekeeping item." He repeated that specific phrase.

Chase had always been disappointed in the two council members who had largely sat quiet while Tacy was berated by the others. However, one of them spoke up and asked for details about the changes.

The response from the city secretary read like it came straight from Tacy's notes:

Previous years' financials showed conflicting numbers and were being revised "for accuracy."

Fuel costs had been "miscategorized" and were now properly recorded.

Funds from the EDC were "accidentally" labeled as state or federal grants.

This got the attention of the other council member who had voted to salvage Tacy's budget the night she quit. He asked how much money was involved in the "housekeeping item."

"$150,000," replied the city secretary.

"You lost $150k?" the council member asked.

"Hold on," another council member interrupted. "We do have $150,000 in expenses we had previously categorized incorrectly, but we offset that with $150,000 in income. It's a wash. We're just cleaning up some minor accounting errors."

"Where'd the income come from?" a council member asked.

"COVID grants. We've been holding some grant money in reserve for specifically this type of event. All very routine," came the answer.

"Why is this coming up now?" a council member asked.

"This is just to tidy up some paperwork for our next audit. Our books are audited. We've passed every audit. That's because we fix the little things like this. We're being transparent here," the city secretary said.

Chase hoped the council would continue to press the issue, but they did not. The routine business of running the town continued until the meeting adjourned.

* * *

The next morning, Chase finished his Americano and walked over to the Beldames' office. The couple was at their shared desk working away, and it was a good chance for Chase to fill them in on the campaign sign problem he had with the city. While he hadn't told anyone about his AirTags, he showed the pair his handy solution. "See?" he asked. He turned his phone towards them and showed them the map.

"You put them all in two places?" Corely asked.

"What?" Chase turned the phone back to himself and, sure enough, there were just two dots. One marked the signs in the bed of his truck. The other marked—"Dang it!"—back at city hall. "City hall has my signs again. Looks like every one of them I put back out is gone."

As he entered city hall, he was greeted by the sight of the usual, lone city employee. No greeting came from her.

"My signs?" he asked.

"Those are evidence. And we have citations for you for each one you put back out," she said.

"For what?" Chase asked.

"The city inspector asked you not to put those back out. And each one you put out after this is a citation as well." She may have stifled a smile.

"The signs are legally marked. I put a sticker on them," Chase said.

She looked at the papers in her hand. "You can take that up with the municipal judge . . . and the court is really backed up. Good luck getting a court date anytime soon."

She handed Chase the papers. Twenty citations. One for every sign he had managed to put back up.

28

Cladoptosis

When all was said and done, Chase's campaign signs were eventually returned. The city attorney had advised that all citations be dropped, and at long last they were. However, city staff took their time doing so. They made Chase show up to municipal court to find out he was in the clear to put his signs back out. He barely got them out in time for election day, which meant he missed most of early voting.

Speaking of missing, Turner Cam didn't appear to see a need for the expense of campaign signs. In fact, he didn't appear to see the need to campaign at all. Maybe he had everyone that mattered in his corner. No one had successfully run against him directly, and he never had a problem getting the people he wanted on city council.

If anyone had seen the mayor, he probably would have boasted that Chase Haven didn't stand a chance, and might have pointed out that his opponent didn't even have the courage to throw an election night watch party. He wouldn't have been wrong. August, Stefan, Corely, and Chase were gathered at the Beldames' small homestead. Chase had decided not to hold a

158

big watch party because he really was worried about losing the election.

It was just this tight group waiting for election results. Stefan had a fancy new grill upon which he reverse-seared some ribeye steaks from "the most expensive beef in Texas."

Meanwhile, the mayor had rented the entire Chamber of Commerce and paid the twenty-five-dollar fee to have the street closed so his party could spill out into the square. It was in the same building that hosted the EDC meetings that the power players would see the mayor win his fourth term. There was some talk in town that his party was BYOB, a move that would upset some of the more conservative churches in town.

Both Max and Diego were at the mayor's party. The two thought it was hilarious. "We're in the lions' den," Max had joked via text message.

As they waited for the polls to close, Corely filled the small group in on all the rumors of the day. Many had noticed that Turner Cam was not up to his old tricks at city hall, the city's only polling place. He was known to greet voters in front of the voting booths and then walk around while they cast their votes. Many didn't want to vote early because of his antics. However, no one had seen him around town since his blowup at the Patrons.

There was a rumor that someone had helped the patients at the local nursing home with their mail-in ballots. Was it Turner Cam? "There's no way someone could get away with that," Stefan said. The rest of the group wasn't so sure.

It was said that the newspaper staff had taken the list of registered voters and marked how they thought each name would vote. No one knew if that was true, but coverage of the election in the paper was almost nonexistent.

Chase couldn't say he had put much effort into his campaign either. Other than the yard signs, his heart just wasn't in it. The only reason he had agreed to run was that maybe being mayor would get him access to the city's files. His open records requests still sat unanswered.

By 7 p.m., the polls closed, and votes were being tallied by the city staff. They'd text the results to all of the city officials as well as the newspaper. First would be the preliminary total from early voting, followed later by the final result.

As the mayor's supporters filed into the Chamber building, they enjoyed the BBQ a loyal restaurant owner had supplied and listened to music playing from a Bluetooth speaker in the corner of the room.

Max texted Chase throughout the night. When the polls closed, Turner Cam was still nowhere to be found. His wife was tending to the guests by herself.

At 8 p.m. Max reported that the building itself was still largely empty, and no one was in the closed street out front. Turner Cam's wife didn't seem to notice the thin crowd, or she simply didn't let it show.

It wasn't long until the text message updates from Max came in rapid-fire. The early voting results were in. Turner's wife stopped the music to announce her husband's early lead. Instead, she stood in silence, staring at her phone.

Then, she walked silently to the building's back room, closed the door behind her, and left her husband's supporters standing in silence.

By this time, the small crowd was beginning to whisper among themselves. Someone found the results posted on Facebook. Chase's small watch party had them too.

Early Vote Total for Mayor
   61 Turner Cam
   110 Chase Haven

The music never played again that night, nor did the crowd grow. Guests were left to chat among themselves, speculating excuses as to why the early results were misleading.

It didn't even take another thirty minutes for the final total to show up on Facebook. When it did, the small group filed out of the building quietly. There'd be no celebration.

Final Vote Total for Mayor
   121 Turner Cam
   219 Chase Haven

When the early voting results came across Facebook, Chase's group may have been more surprised than even Turner Cam. They had talked about Chase's support within the congregation of St. Stephen, but they had all doubted that the mayor could be beaten. Chase assumed the positive reception he got around town was just typical Texas politeness.

Once the small group calmed down, August focused them on the challenge ahead. "They're going to say that you beating Turner Cam undermines your claim that the town is run by a good old boy club."

"I don't care about any of that. I'm going to crawl through every inch of that building until I find out exactly what happened to Tacy," Chase said.

Corely said, "I heard that the office staff at city hall bragged about quitting their jobs if you won. You could be walking into a building of empty offices."

"You might have a bigger problem than that," August said. "Did people vote for you, or were they simply voting against Turner Cam? You've got to win over the town, and I'd start with the big families that stayed quiet during all of this."

"Like who?" Chase asked.

"There are only maybe half a dozen families with any real money and influence around here. The only thing they have in common is that they would never openly attack someone. They always solve their disagreements quietly and usually through an intermediary. Turner Cam was just a tool to be used, and now he's no longer useful," Corely said.

Stefan added his own thoughts, as only he could. "Have you ever heard of cladoptosis? That's when a tree self-prunes. It will just let go of a branch that's sick or not getting enough sunlight. Those trees we have out front with the pink flowers are desert willow. They'll self-prune just like this town and its most powerful families. No one is losing their grip on the town. They just dropped Turner Cam like a sick branch."

"If there are six families running the town, I can only count one that the mayor did the bidding of—the Whiteys. What were the other five families doing?" Chase asked.

"Watching you settle the score."

29

Secretary of State

Chase parked his truck outside city hall and walked inside. It was noon on a weekday, and there weren't many cars. Upon entering, Chase was greeted by the sight of the photographer from the paper, the entire city council, the three city office employees, and a small audience taking their seats.

Chase timed his arrival so he could slip into a seat right as the meeting began. He didn't even look to the crowd. He was nervous, and he didn't want to talk to anyone. He was mostly avoiding whatever passive aggressive statements the town's leaders would make and the thin veil of politeness they'd hide behind. He was relieved to see the city council assembled when he opened the door. The mayor pro tem, a city council member who had the task of filling in for the absent Turner Cam, gaveled the meeting into order just as Chase took his seat. Turner Cam was nowhere to be seen.

Chase paid attention to the meeting despite hearing the words "rubber stamp" repeated in his head. This time it really was a rubber stamp. The city office staff, who acted as the town's election officials, were legally required to certify the results of the election. That's what Stefan had said anyway. It didn't matter how they felt. They would likely present the vote totals to the city council on a single sheet of paper. The whole event would take less than five minutes. They would then recess the meeting to swear in their new mayor. Chase assumed he'd put his hand on a Bible and promise to "preserve, protect, and defend" and so on.

The mayor pro tem asked the city staff to approach the podium and walked them through certifying the election results. The three women who were the entirety of the city office staff went to the podium together. The one who seemed like the one in charge was the city secretary. She spoke for the group. She was joined by the city treasurer. The final person to walk to the podium was the interim city manager, a woman that had gone from answering the phones to filling in for Aaron Foster in the span of a five-minute emergency meeting of the city council.

"Good afternoon," the city secretary began. "I have in my hand letters of resignation from the three of us standing before you today. They're effective immediately."

Click. Click. Click. The photographer from the paper was capturing the moment.

The three women turned and walked towards the door without another word. They had their backs to Chase, who briefly wondered if they had smiles on their faces.

The city council, who appeared to Chase to wear expressions of genuine surprise, looked to the city attorney. He responded by leaning towards his microphone and speaking. "We're going to need a recess."

The mayor pro tem pounded the gavel against a wood block on the table in front of him. "We're adjourned."

The city attorney walked to Aaron Foster's old office alone and closed the door behind him. The council members stood and at first appeared to mill about aimlessly. Slowly, they shared quiet words with each other. Chase was watching intently, but couldn't make out what they were saying. It looked like a game of telephone, with messages going from members at the end of the table down the line to the mayor pro tem. Eventually, he left to join the city attorney in Foster's old office.

Chase finally noticed Stefan and Corely were standing over his shoulder. They must have been watching the exchanges between the council members as closely as he was. That or they didn't want to disturb him. Chase stood and turned towards them. The three of them formed something of a circle.

"What was that?" Corely asked.

"Exactly what was predicted," Chase said.

"I didn't think they'd actually do it—especially before certifying the results. That might be illegal," Stefan said.

"You think?" Chase raised an eyebrow towards Stefan.

"I don't know. Where's August and his boys?"

"Work. Some contract somewhere."

As the minutes ticked by, the crowd spoke amongst themselves. Some came by to shake Chase's hand and to ask if he knew what was going on or if he saw it coming.

"No." That is all he said.

Everyone went back to their seats when the city attorney reappeared. It had been over an hour of recess. The mayor pro tem gaveled them back into session.

"Okay," he said. "The secretary of state is going to name new election officials. That's going to take some time. Until then, we continue as-is. This body is going to call an emergency meeting to appoint new staff for the roles of city secretary, city manager, and city treasurer. They'll fill those roles until this council names permanent replacements. Our public works staff are still operating. We rely on a private company for trash service and water billing. We do not anticipate any disruptions in city services. However, we do ask for the public's patience when calling city hall as we get things sorted out."

"Where is Turner Cam during all of this?" a man shouted from the audience.

"You're out of order, sir. We aren't taking any questions. The city attorney has advised me that we will have no further discussion until an emergency meeting is called to appoint new staff."

The mayor pro tem paused and looked around the room before banging his gavel. "Having no further business before us, we are adjourned."

The city council members, as a group, shot up from their chairs and bolted for the private exit, the same one Tacy had disappeared through some weeks ago. The audience was left with no one to answer questions. Chase stood and walked to the same door. He opened it to find it was just a small, empty room with a door on the opposite wall. As the door to the council chambers shut behind him, he opened the other door to find himself in the city parking lot. This is where city vehicles parked, closed off to the public.

There, talking among themselves, stood the city council. "What am I supposed to do?" Chase asked no one in particular.

The city attorney responded, "You can take office after the state certifies the election."

"When is that?" Chase asked.

"Weeks . . . months. We don't know if this has ever happened before," a city council member replied.

"And what am I supposed to do?" Chase asked.

"You're a private citizen until then," the attorney said. He turned away from Chase and faced the council members.

"And Turner Cam?" Chase asked.

The city attorney turned back around, as if to make the point that Chase was being a pest. "He's still mayor." He turned back to the others.

"If he ever shows back up for work." Chase went back through the door and reentered the council chambers. It was empty other than Stefan and Corely. Chase could see some of the audience outside through the glass door.

"What happened?" Stefan asked.

Chase didn't answer. Instead, he walked over to the closed door of Aaron Foster's old office, opened it, and stepped inside.

Empty.

"The files are gone," he said.

"Think the sheriff has them?" Stefan asked.

"No idea. Let's get out of here." Chase relayed his brief conversation with the city attorney and council to Stefan and Corely as they all walked to the Butterfield for a beer.

30

Pump Station

Chase pulled out of the alley behind his apartment determined to track down Whip and ask about the whereabouts of Aaron Foster's files. He barely made it past the downtown square before he pulled off the road alongside a pickup with "Supervisor" printed under the city logo on the door. Next to it was a septic tank truck with "We're #1 in #2" in bold red letters on the side. But it wasn't either of those trucks that had caught his attention. It was Whip's cruiser.

A city employee, a man in work coveralls, and Whip were standing on a concrete pad nearby. Chase approached the three men. "What's going on?"

"We have sewage backed up in this part of the system and assumed the screen was clogged, which isn't unusual. We had started to pump out this wet well when we found it," the city worker said.

"It's a body," the pump truck operator added.

"Let's get a better look," Whip said. He started to move towards the opening.

The city worker grabbed Whip's arm. "Hold on. You fall

in that hole, and there'll be two bodies to fish out. There's methane and hydrogen sulfide down there, plus biohazards you can't even pronounce."

Whip stopped. "Okay, but I need to lay eyes on it."

The city worker got Whip suited up in what he called "PPE," or personal protective equipment. It consisted of a hard hat, eyewear, and a safety harness with a tether. Even with this, he could only peer over the side of the opening. At least twelve feet below, poorly illuminated by a work lamp, appeared to be a human body. Whip snapped a photo with his phone.

Once safely away from the pump station wet well opening, Whip was able to zoom in on the photo on his phone. Chase looked over his shoulder at the photo. It still wasn't possible to make out who it was. In fact, it was impossible to tell if it was even male or female.

"How can I get a better look?" Whip asked the city employee.

"We need to get a detector down there. We have to check for oxygen content, then combustibles, and then toxins. Once the other truck gets here, we'll grab the multi-gas sensor off of it and let you know."

"Okay, get to it," Whip said. He turned towards Chase, but before he could speak the city employee spoke again.

"The access hatch was locked. I swear by it. Somebody had to have a key to open it and a key to close it."

Whip, who had turned back towards the man, appeared to be agitated. Chase assumed that statement wasn't something the sheriff wanted shared with anyone, maybe especially Chase. "Thanks," Whip said.

He turned back to Chase. "Get out of here. There are more reporters in town than ever," Whip then put his hand on Chase's shoulder. "Hold on. The state is going to take this over. If this is what we think it is, I'll let you know. I'm sorry."

"Okay."

* * *

Chase left the scene and drove to the hunting cabin. He found
Max waiting on the porch with a soft-sided cooler, which he
placed in the bed of the truck. Max climbed into the passenger
seat silently.

All Chase had said on the phone was, "I'm thinking about
driving out to Castle Gap." Max had replied, "I'll be ready in
five."

Chase followed the route taken by Aaron Foster his last day
on earth. They turned left to McCamey and then followed the
highway to Castle Gap Road.

When Chase brought the truck to a stop outside the locked
gate, Max hopped out and opened the gate.

It didn't look like anyone was around, but the two could have
been followed by a fleet of trucks and Chase probably wouldn't
have noticed.

Chase drove through the gate before Max closed it and jumped
back in the truck.

"That's a dummy lock. It isn't even keyed. 'Not-a-lock' I
think they call them. Looks real but isn't. Anyone could come
in and out if they knew about it," Max said.

Chase nodded, but didn't reply.

He drove the truck up to the same abandoned pad site where
Aaron Foster had parked. He put the cooler strap over one
shoulder and started walking towards the gap. Max followed.

After climbing out of the first draw to the top of a rise, Chase
opened the cooler, handed Max a beer, and took one for himself.

"Okay. What are we doing out here?" Max asked as he opened his beer.

"Clearing my head, I think." Chase cracked open his beer. "Tacy liked it out here." He took a sip. "Maybe we missed something."

"The sheriff was all over this place," Max said.

"Aaron and Turner did what? Followed her out here?" Chase asked. He began walking again. "Why not leave her body out here?"

"I'm guessing they did."

"Nah, she was found today. In town. Stuffed in a well. State will confirm it at some point."

Max didn't reply. The two hiked for several minutes in silence.

"It was a locked well. Aaron Foster would have had a key," Chase said.

"Why would they take her all the way back to town?"

Chase stopped. As he turned to look at Max, he heard the report of a rifle in the distance. They both dove to the ground at the unmistakable sound of a bullet ricocheting off the rocks nearby.

31

Chihuahuan Desert

On the easternmost edge of the Chihuahuan Desert, Max and Chase found themselves face down in the dirt hugging rocks.

"Where did that shot come from?" Chase asked.

"Somewhere near the truck, maybe. I'm not sticking my head up to find out," Max replied.

Pinned down on a rise in the shadow of Castle Gap, they had heard the unmistakable sound of gunfire. A single shot.

"A rifle for sure," Max said.

Chase knew that the round was meant for them.

"We can't stay here. They've either run off or they're circling around to get a better shot," Chase said.

"Or they're waiting for you to stick your head up," Max said.

Chase did stick his head up, but as little as necessary to get a clear view of the truck. It was sitting alone on the pad site where they had left it.

"Truck is still there. Let's back into this draw and take it around," Chase suggested.

The two backtracked on their bellies towards a low draw closer to the gap. Once Chase felt confident he was out of sight of the shooter, he stood up.

"Which way?" Max asked.

Chase took a coin from his pocket, flipped it low in the air, caught it, and held it against his wrist.

"You can't be serious," Max said.

"Heads we go that way," Chase said, nodding in one direction down the draw, and removed the hand that had been concealing the coin against his wrist. It was tails. "Easy enough."

The draw had a subtle bend to it, which gave the impression that it continued on much farther than it did. It was only a few hundred feet before it forced them to climb—and reveal themselves to the shooter—once again.

Chase went first, poking his head just high enough to get a glimpse of the truck again. He then retreated the few feet back to Max. "I don't see another car anywhere out here. Whoever it is came some distance on foot," Chase said.

"We make a run for it? To the truck?"

"I'm in good standing with God." Chase cast a sarcastic smile in Max's direction. "So maybe I go first."

"Somebody took a shot at us. Maybe now isn't the time for a foxhole conversation about Jesus," Max said. He did not return the smile.

"The way I figure it—" Chase popped his head up again and scanned the area while speaking. "I'm about to jump up and run to that truck. When I take my last breath, I'll know that my next one will be with Tacy . . . all because some old German Lutheran lady invited her to church and then Tacy invited me."

Chase didn't wait for a reply. Staying as low to the ground as he could, he ran over the top of the rise and back down into a draw on the other side, closer to the truck.

He then crouched quietly in the bottom of the draw, looking

back in the direction from which he had come.

Max's head appeared over the rise. He was just high enough to get a good look around. Once he had thoroughly scanned the area, he hopped to his feet and ran the same path as Chase.

Once in the draw, the two followed it, which led them closer to the road. It went a considerable distance until only flat ground remained between them and the truck.

"That's a lot of ground to cover, man," Max said.

Chase stood up and, without a word, sprinted towards the truck. It was easily three football fields of open ground. Nothing above knee height grew in the area.

Max drew his pistol and knelt in place, scanning the area.

When Chase reached the truck, he leaned against it and caught his breath as he scanned the area. Max holstered his pistol and followed the path Chase had taken.

When Max reached the truck, he faced the opposite direction as Chase and scanned the horizon. "I haven't even seen a rattlesnake out here, much less a person."

"No car either," Chase said. "Maybe it was just a hunter?"

"Deer season is over. We would have seen a car go out towards the highway. Let's take the truck up the road the other way and look around," Max said.

Chase started the truck and looked over his shoulder as he put it in reverse. He backed the truck in a wide circle until they were facing the road they came in on.

"Let's go up the road farther—away from the highway," Max repeated.

Chase put the truck in drive and turned right off the pad site.

Castle Gap Road snaked around King Mountain, and Chase kept the speed low enough to prevent a towering cloud of dust from forming behind the truck. Max scanned the area on his side of the truck while Chase kept an eye out his window.

They slowed anytime they crossed an intersection. The short roads feeding various pad sites were replaced by ones going into the solar and wind farms that dominated the other side of the mountain.

"More ostriches," Chase remarked involuntarily.

"What?"

"Never mind. I don't even see any workers out here. We should have hustled back to the truck faster. Whoever took a shot at us must be long gone."

Eventually, the road joined Highway 349 and Chase took a right, which led him to the small town of Rankin and then back through McCamey. As the pair left McCamey, Chase's phone rang from its holder on the dash. He pressed the green icon and then put the call on speaker.

"Whip?"

"The lab results are back."

"Oh . . . what we thought?"

"No."

"What do you mean *no*?"

"It wasn't Tacy."

Max interrupted, "Then who?"

"Who is that?!" Whip asked.

"It's Max," Chase replied.

Chase could hear him exhale over the phone. "Come by the office. Alone. Please," Whip said before hanging up.

32

Handshake

Chase dropped Max off at the Running AB and then drove straight to the sheriff's office. As he entered the building, Whip stuck his head out of his office and waved for Chase to join him. Once Chase was through the doorway, Whip signaled for him to close the door and take a seat.

"It's Turner Cam."

"What?"

"The body. It's the mayor—the previous mayor."

Chase's mouth fell open. "How long's he been in there?"

"They can't be sure. That environment down there . . . they said it decomposed him so fast they can't estimate when he was put there, but he was put there."

"Do they know what killed him?"

"He's all there. His body is intact, but they can't tell what killed him."

"Can you tell me when the last time was anyone saw him?"

"The second time you put him in the hospital—when you went to his office. When they tried to discharge him from the hospital, no one came up there to pick him up. One of my deputies gave him a ride home and his wife wouldn't let him in. We left him at the motel."

"What do you mean she wouldn't let him in?" Chase asked.

"The deputy couldn't hear what she said, but rumor is that she didn't show her face in town after his outburst at the Patrons. Him having another run-in with you was probably the last straw for that marriage."

Whip had a full coffee pot on a little credenza against the wall. Chase walked over and started to pour himself a cup. "She was at his election party."

"Sure, but he wasn't. She was just keeping up appearances. And, he wasn't in the motel anymore either. They said he paid for a week up front and then they never saw him again."

Chase returned to his seat with a partially full Styrofoam cup. "The press is going to eat this up."

"Right." Whip got up and walked over to the coffee pot.

"I can't be anywhere near this."

"I agree," Whip said. He poured himself a coffee in his own mug, white with the star of the sheriff's department. "This town doesn't need any more bad press."

"I hate to add to your worries," Chase said. "Somebody took a shot at me and Max today."

"Where?"

"We were out at Castle Gap. Never saw them, much less a car or truck. One shot hit somewhere near us while we were hiking the gap."

"I'll look into it." Whip took a sip of his coffee.

Chase, suddenly thinking better of drinking coffee at this hour, set his cup down untouched.

"You know Turner Cam killed Tacy," Chase said.

"Probably, but the town doesn't think that, and the state

can't prove he was involved."

"He was in the truck, Whip! Aaron Foster and Turner Cam followed her out of town after the meeting, killed her, and burned their own truck to hide the evidence!" Chase did make a sincere effort to control his volume.

"Why didn't they burn her truck? So that Aaron Foster could lead you back to the scene later?" Whip crossed his arms.

Chase clenched his jaw. "Let the Texas Rangers solve this one, Whip."

"This is why people take shots at you." Whip uncrossed his arms and leaned forward. "You're too stupid to read the room. I'm trying to help you, but I'm in the facts business not the feelings business. I don't get to go around taking a swing at anyone I think is involved."

"Turner Cam didn't stuff himself in a pump station and then lock it."

"Who did it, Chase? What's your crackpot theory? I can't wait to hear what you and that amateur private detective over at August's ranch think." Whip stood. "Please say Baxter Whitey." Whip walked around his desk and leaned into Chase's face. "Go take a swing at Baxter Whitey and see what that gets you. He's easy to find. He's either playing with his airplane or at the bottom of a bottle at that pilots' lounge."

"Maybe I will" was what Chase wanted to say, but he stopped himself. He took a deep breath. He tried to force himself to relax. "Whip." He let out a loud exhale. "I saw a city truck follow Tacy out of town." Whip leaned back as Chase continued. "That same night, a city truck just happens to catch on fire with the mayor and city manager driving it? And when I confront the city manager, he loses his cool and drives straight to Tacy's car and stabs me with a lit road flare."

"Yeah—"

"No, hold on," Chase said. "And the mayor summons me to his office. Oh, and that's after he lost his ever-loving mind at the Patrons. My guess is that's what the stress of murdering someone will do to a guy." Chase straightened in his seat and leaned forward towards Whip just slightly. "That night, the night I put Turner Cam in the hospital for the second time, I told Rebecca Whitey that Turner Cam flipped on them."

"Flipped on them how?" There was a hint of something in the sheriff's voice. Sarcasm? No. Skepticism.

"I told her that Turner Cam gave me notes from a meeting. A meeting between Scout Commercial Partners, Turner Cam, Aaron Foster, and Baxter Whitey."

"What did they say?"

"The airport project. It laid out all the demands from Scout Commercial Partners. They'd get a bunch of tax breaks and incentives from the city and EDC. In exchange, they'd take some of that money to buy Baxter's land at a huge premium."

"And the mayor just gave you this?"

"Not exactly, but I told Rebecca he did. I told her he wanted out."

"Not exactly?"

"The notes are real, but he didn't give them to me. They were on his computer. He was . . . resting his eyes when I took a quick look at it."

Whip straightened. "I thought we were being honest with each other." He walked back around his desk and sat in his chair. "An elected official was found stuffed in a pump station . . ."

"I'll give you the notes."

"What notes?"

"Off Turner Cam's computer. They spell it all out."

"I don't know about notes. Don't know what you're talking about." Whip stood from his chair again.

"And the gunshot today?" Chase asked.

"I'll look into it." Whip walked around his desk.

"That's it?"

"You were trespassing."

"That's got to be someone telling us to back off," Chase said.

"An incredibly stupid somebody, or perhaps they just wanted you off their land," Whip said.

He folded his arms and leaned back against the corner of his desk. "You physically assaulted an elected official, not once but twice, and now he's found dead. Surely you understand you're a suspect here."

"Then I'd like a lawyer."

"You're not under arrest. You're free to go." Whip motioned towards the door before recrossing his arms.

"I just want to find out what happened to Tacy. That's all I've ever wanted. Where are Aaron Foster's files?"

"That's a dead end. There's nothing there."

"And the city computers?"

"Nothing."

"Nothing as in wiped clean, or nothing as in no clues?"

"Look, today wasn't a courtesy update." Whip uncrossed his arms and straightened.

Chase stood. "Alright. I'm leaving."

"Good idea."

33

Terminal Event

Chase sat on the porch of August's hunting cabin with Max. Sarah was inside preparing for August, Stefan, and Corely to arrive.

Max and Sarah still hadn't found a place to buy in town. The hunting cabin was home for now.

A bottle of Empire Rye sat on a small table between the two. The view did little to fight off Chase's somber mood. The EDC wasn't the only one looking at an empty bank account. Chase was barely making ends meet selling eggs, flipping guns, and renting the flower shop.

The town was abuzz with the news that Turner Cam was dead. Stefan and Corely fed Chase every version of the story making its way through town. It was no secret that the remains were found by city workers during routine maintenance, the former mayor was identified through DNA analysis, and they didn't know when or how he died.

What nobody was talking about was Tacy. Her case had long since been solved in the minds of many when Aaron Foster was shot. Chase wasn't even sure what justice looked like anymore. An earlier phone call from Shy-Anne asking for an update had become a regular exercise in frustration. He didn't have an update. He just hoped Max wouldn't spend the evening rehashing all of the dead ends he had just laid out on the phone to Shy-Anne.

Maybe they could just enjoy the view. August owned the horizon, and at this time of day, that paid dividends. A blood-red sun hung heavy in the sky. Chase would be okay to stare right at it and watch it wave goodbye to the day.

"Turner Cam?" Chase said.

Max turned his head towards Chase.

"That wet well was basically outside the back door of city hall," Chase added. "We should buy whoever took out the trash a beer or something."

Max nodded his head, agreeing with Chase's assessment.

They sat for a moment.

"Some of the things we did . . ." Chase started. He didn't finish his thought.

Max looked back at him as he took a sip of his drink. He then looked back out at the sunset and raised his glass as if to salute the sun.

The world around them was washed in red.

"There really are no heroes, Chase."

"Yeah. At best you'll find a few good fellows—*bon camarade*." Chase didn't raise his glass. A vehicle approaching from the distance caught his attention. "Who's that?"

"Not Stefan and Corely," Max said.

A fairly new pickup. White. Common. It wasn't clear who was driving the truck until it stopped and the lone occupant got out.

"Brady Laye," Chase said. He only spoke loud enough for

Max to hear.

Max didn't respond.

"Gentlemen," Brady said.

"How goes it?" Chase asked.

"Just fine. How are you fellas?" Brady asked.

"Just fine. What can we do for you?" Max asked.

"I got something I think you should know."

"Oh yeah?"

"Yeah." He nodded. "A fella is running around town shooting his mouth off about you."

"That can't be too unusual," Chase said.

"Maybe not, but this one was at my place bragging about getting off work to go celebrate."

"What was he celebrating?" Max asked.

"Baxter Whitey signed a lease for a gas pipeline to cross one of his ranches to the rendering plant near Girvin. The county commissioners made sure the deal got a big tax break. Renewable natural gas, they call it. They'll capture gas off the plant and sell it into the pipeline. The guy wouldn't shut up about it."

"What's a rendering plant?" Max asked.

"It's like a recycling plant for animal waste, cooking grease, and such. They make all sorts of products that go into fertilizers and animal feed."

"You going to tell us who you're talking about?" Chase asked.

"Does the last name Bird ring a bell with you?" Brady asked.

"Yeah, the city secretary that was supposed to certify my election is a Bird."

"That's her husband, Cody. He drives the truck for the rendering plant, but he says that this new project will earn him a big promotion. He's a talker. Got a big mouth. He talks my ear off every time he comes to pick up at my place."

"Sounds like a winner," Max said.

"He's trouble. Has been his whole life. He said they're going to run you out of town," Brady said.

"That's a new one," Chase said.

"The thing that got me, other than that he said 'they,' is he stuck his finger out when he said it and made a little shooting gesture." Brady pointed his index finger at Chase and bent his thumb to mimic the action.

Chase leaned forward in his chair. "What do you think he meant?"

"Rumor is that somebody took a shot at you."

"It isn't a rumor," Max said.

"Well, I don't know what the guy is capable of or what he might do next. My guess is something big, and something soon. I just didn't want it on my conscience," Brady said.

"Do you believe Baxter Whitey is behind this? Is Bird their guy or something?" Max asked.

"I'm not saying anything. I was never here." Brady slapped his leg. He stepped up on the porch and extended his hand to Chase. "Bird starts his route at the rendering plant each morning." Chase returned the handshake.

"Thanks for coming out," Max said as he shook Brady's hand. Brady ducked into his truck and left.

34

Trash Bag

Chase pulled off the highway down a well-maintained road, just wide enough for two large trucks to pass. He hugged the shoulder as an oncoming oil field truck sped past him without letting off the gas. He was left to navigate through a cloud of dust as he edged closer to the Girvin Rendering Plant.

The plant itself, which was growing larger as he got closer, was one expansive building and three towering tanks. The metallic tanks dully reflected the morning sun's light.

As he pulled up in front of the facility, Chase saw one large roll-up door to the building standing open. There was activity inside, but only the first few feet inside the door were visible. The bright morning sun overpowered whatever lights were on, leaving the inside of the building in relative darkness. Chase parked his truck next to a few others neatly lined up against a fence just feet away from the open door.

He opened his door and stepped out. The smell hit him immediately. It was earthy, but foul. He could almost feel it. It made him involuntarily squint and wrinkle his nose.

Four large trucks sat with their cargo doors open, dripping

with liquid. Green garden hoses laid sprawled across the ground behind them. There was no one in sight outside the building.

Once Chase crossed the yard and into the threshold of the open door, his eyes adjusted to the change in light, and he stopped dead in his tracks. Standing before him were four adult men in a semicircle around an open case of beer that laid at their feet. What caught him off guard wasn't the men or their breakfast beers. It was how they were dressed.

Each of the four men was wearing a black trash bag.

They clearly had nothing else above the waist. The large black bags were cut with holes for their heads and arms. It was the strangest thing Chase had ever seen. He had come to the plant to confront Cody Bird. He'd told himself he was ready for anything. He had even thought he might see Baxter Whitey himself and rehearsed what he would say and do.

He was wrong. He wasn't prepared for four men in trash bags. Whatever this was, it was a first for Chase.

Chase's brain was on high alert as he took in the sight. Clearly these men were not bothered by the smell. Dirty water dripped off their trash bag shirts, creating rings on the floor around where they each stood. Wet gloves laid at their feet.

Chase had a good guess who one of the men was. He had seen him around town before. He was the only one of the four he recognized, and the look on the man's face suggested he also recognized Chase.

That had to be Cody Bird. Chase's thoughts went to the pistol hiding under his shirt in his waistband.

The man smiled. "Grab him!"

Cody shoved his hands into Chase's chest, but Chase was quick enough to step to his right, avoiding most of the force. He grabbed Cody by the shirt—or trash bag—with his right hand

and drove his left elbow into Cody's face. That should have been a blow that sent Cody to the floor. One shot. However, the trash bag ripped in Chase's hand, which robbed his blow of most of its power.

Cody didn't slow to inspect the blood pouring from his nose thanks to Chase's elbow. Most men would have paused to assess the damage. Not Cody. He was all offense. Chase brought his left arm, the one that had just struck Cody's nose, up against his own head to absorb a wide-arcing right from Cody. A left hand, a haymaker strong enough to knock a man out, came next. Chase brought his right arm up to absorb that blow. He knew he couldn't take many of those. Even with his arm over his head, the blows were jarring. Chase responded with a left uppercut planted deep in Cody's soft belly. It hit its mark. The man, clearly too focused on delivering his own blows to brace himself, went to the ground.

As Bird went down, one of the other men tackled Chase. Chase tried his best to protect his head on the way to the concrete. He quickly found himself on his back looking up at another one of the men kneeling down to deliver a punch to his face. Chase protected his head as the group went to work on him.

Chase knew to keep his eyes open and look for an opportunity, but there was none. The man who tackled him was holding him down while the other two went to work on his upper and lower body. The pain was almost overwhelming.

As suddenly as it began, it stopped. Chase had his arms over his face. His eyes were open. It only took him a moment to come to grips with the situation. He quickly learned why they had stopped.

His own pistol had been taken from his holster and was pointed at his face.

Chase would pay the ultimate price for being indecisive. He should have drawn his gun and shot Cody Bird, but he let the man get too close. He'd brought a gun to a fistfight and didn't use it.

Chase had a clear image of his final moments. At least he'd soon be with Tacy. That was the promise when he went to church with her. A grown man in a robe poured water on his head. Undeserved favor is what the pastor called his baptism. Then every week that same pastor would tell him he was forgiven. Chase only went to church for Tacy, but he'd have given anything to be there in that moment. He needed to hear that he was forgiven. Instead, he was staring at his own gun.

The man above him turned his gaze towards the door. Chase turned his head to see a man outlined by the bright sun.

The men held their hands up in surrender. Except the one who didn't. The one with Chase's pistol kept it trained on the shadow in the door and fired first. The sound was deafening. Chase's ears began to ring.

Through the ringing Chase could hear a second shot. It was return fire from the doorway.

Chase grabbed the gun. He forced the barrel up into the man's chest and the two began their struggle.

The other three, which included Cody Bird, didn't wait around to see what happened next. They ran deep into the building.

Chase raised his hips and rolled left. The man, using both hands to control the gun, couldn't stop himself from toppling over and suddenly finding Chase on top of him.

Chase drove his shoulder into the man's neck and used both hands to wrestle the gun away but dropped it in the struggle. It was like the man he was wrestling with had suddenly let go, which caught Chase off guard.

Chase sat up, but his attacker didn't move. That's when Chase saw the blood. The man had been shot and bled out during their struggle.

Chase turned towards the door. There was Max, the figure in the door. He was now lying on the ground holding his leg. Chase didn't break stride. If Max had taken a round to his upper thigh, he could have seconds before he bled out. Chase ran right past him and out the door.

Into the glaring morning sun, Chase made it to his truck, opened the door, and grabbed his first aid kit. He turned and was back to Max within seconds.

Chase didn't speak. He ripped open the hook and loop closure of his first aid bag and grabbed his tourniquet.

Max was trying his best to apply pressure to the wound on his leg.

Chase opened the tourniquet and wrapped it around Max's leg, a few inches above the blood gushing out around Max's hands. There was so much blood.

Chase buckled the strap together and pulled, tightening the tourniquet as far as it went.

35

Windlass Rod

Chase turned the windlass rod on the tourniquet to tighten it even further—painfully tight judging by Max's wince. Chase used the tourniquet's clip to secure the rod in place.

Scissors from the first aid kit allowed him to cut the material around the wound and finally get a good look at it. He stuffed the wound, which had mostly stopped bleeding, and put Max's hands over the fresh gauze. "Keep pressure on this while I call for help."

Max grabbed Chase's phone from his hand. Through the ringing in his ears came Max's voice. "I've got this. Don't let him get away."

Chase looked up to see a pickup speeding out of the yard. It was too far ahead for him to catch. As he thought of pursuing it, a more attractive target appeared.

A second pickup, with a lone occupant, was backing out of a space. It was Cody Bird, and Chase could catch him.

"I can—" Chase turned back to Max. He was no longer sitting up. He had slumped back on his elbows and then slid flat on the ground. He was staring up at the ceiling of the large metal building.

Any thought of pursuing Cody left Chase's mind in that frightening instant.

Just as quickly, a wave of relief washed over Chase when he spotted the rise and fall of Max's chest. He was breathing. Any thought of pursuing Cody, for whatever crumb of justice could be found there, had completely left Chase's mind.

That's when he heard a woman's voice.

"Sit tight. Don't move."

The man he had wrestled with still lay dead on the floor. Chase's gun, no longer laying innocently nearby, was in the hands of the exact last person Chase expected to see in that warehouse.

It was Rebecca Whitey, and for the second time that day, Chase found himself staring down the barrel of his own pistol.

Chase raised his hands with open palms facing her.

"Stand up and kick that gun over here." She motioned with the barrel of Chase's own gun towards Max's pistol.

Chase stood, rested the toe of his boot against Max's gun, and kicked it towards Rebecca. It slid to a stop against the body of the man she stood over.

"Clean slate, I think you called it," Rebecca said, gun still trained on Chase.

"Ma'am?"

"Clean slate. That's what you said when you and Stefan harangued me in your apartment."

Chase could not take his eyes off the gun in her hand.

"You had every chance to walk away," she continued.

"Walk away from Tacy's murder?" Chase asked.

"You"—she pushed the gun towards Chase to accentuate the word—"you didn't run for mayor for that girl. You did it to kill the airport deal. To attack my family. To destroy what I've built."

"I did it to find out what really happened to Tacy."

"She was killed by two idiots. Tolerating them was the cost of doing business—of getting things done around here." Rebecca's voice was steady. "Now they're both dead, which should have ended this. That was your clean slate."

Chase was too far away from Rebecca to make any play for the gun. "Those two men getting killed makes everything even?"

"That's right."

"You killed Turner Cam to put an end to this?"

"No . . . you did." Rebecca reached into her pocket with her free hand and withdrew a white cloth, from which she dropped a small metallic object. The brass-colored item hit the concrete floor with a ring. She kicked it over to Chase.

As the object slid towards his feet, it became obvious to Chase what it was.

A key.

"Pick it up." She took one step closer to Chase, pointing the pistol at the key and then back at him.

"Pick it up."

Chase bent over and picked up the key.

"Put it in your pocket."

Chase complied.

"Don't worry. Help is on the way for all of us. I called 9-1-1 the second you broke into my business and shot my employee for trying to stop you."

"Your business." Chase delivered it as a statement not a question.

"You thought that I'm just the dutiful housewife?"

The unmistakable sound of tires crunching over gravel filled the warehouse, but Chase didn't turn around. He kept his hands up and eyes focused on the gun pointed at him.

"Sheriff Dantonio," Rebecca said.

"Chase, are you armed?" Whip asked. He stood behind Chase.

"No, sir," Chase said.

"Rebecca, please lower your gun, place it on the ground, and take three steps to your left."

"Can I help Max?" Chase asked. His hands were still raised.

"Hold on," Whip said. He patted down Chase's sides and midsection. "Okay. Go ahead."

Chase knelt next to Max. He was breathing, but it was definitely shallower than it had been. His eyes were closed.

A second cruiser pulled up. A young deputy stepped out. "Deputy, please put Mrs. Whitey in the front seat of your rig. We'll get her statement once we get this man some help."

Whip turned back to Chase. "There's an ambulance coming right behind me."

Rebecca walked past the two men as they looked over Max. "Thank you, Sheriff. I—" She stopped midsentence.

Chase looked up at her but couldn't see her face as the young deputy gently nudged her on towards his cruiser.

"What's that?" Whip asked.

Chase turned his head back to Whip and then followed his eyes down to Max's hand.

In it was Chase's smartphone. "The screen's on."

"Please wait here, ma'am," Chase heard the young deputy say. Chase looked over his shoulder and saw that the young deputy had placed Rebecca in the front passenger seat of his cruiser.

"I think he's recording," Whip said. Chase looked back at the phone in Max's hand. The screen showed an image of the warehouse.

"Put this one in my car," Whip said to the young deputy as he nodded towards Chase.

"Whip, you've got to watch that video," Chase said.

"Go," Whip said. He then looked to his young deputy. "I think we need a helicopter for this guy."

The young deputy grabbed Chase's shoulder and walked him over to Whip's cruiser. He held open the passenger door as Chase climbed inside. "Please wait here, sir, and we'll come back and get your statement."

Chase sat in the cruiser and watched as the ambulance arrived. Two EMTs emerged and began to work on Max.

Chase tried his best to watch, but he couldn't tell what they were doing. Soon, Whip appeared in the doorway and walked towards him.

Whip opened the door of the cruiser, sat inside, and started the engine. He closed his door as the young deputy walked past them towards his own car.

"Is he okay?" Chase asked.

"He's breathing on his own. I'd say that's pretty good considering." Whip put the cruiser in reverse, looked over the seat, and began to back up. "We need to make space for the chopper."

"Did you look at the video?" Chase asked.

"That can wait."

"Max recorded that while he was bleeding to death over there. Give it one minute. It'll show you who you really have in that other car."

"Okay, but this is on the record." Whip took his audio recorder out of his pocket, flipped it on, and set it on the dashboard between them. The red light glowed at Chase as he unpacked the morning's events.

The other cruiser backed up next to them. Chase could see Rebecca. Her sharp eyes were intently watching the two of them from the other car.

Whip held up Chase's phone far out in front of them enough for him to see the screen as Chase navigated through it. Just beyond Whip, Chase could see the young deputy leave his cruiser. He caught a glimpse of Rebecca again. Chase felt as if she was looking right through them.

The young deputy walked over to the ambulance and began moving it between the cruisers and the open rendering plant door, creating a large open space in the middle of the yard.

Chase continued to manipulate the phone, but he couldn't find any recent video. If didn't help that the phone was being held by Whip or that he was also trying to tell his version of events as he went. Rebecca, tight-jawed, remained directly in his line of sight.

A distant sound, like the roll of a drum, signaled the impending arrival of the helicopter. "Sit tight," Whip said.

"Hold on!" Chase interjected.

"There's nothing on here, Chase." Whip exited his cruiser with Chase's phone in hand and walked through the open rendering plant door.

The sound of the approaching helicopter quickly morphed from distant thunder to an intimidating storm of dust. The sound of gravel bouncing off the cruiser faded as the helicopter touched down.

As two flight medics jumped out with a stretcher, Chase looked over at the young deputy's cruiser.

The front passenger door was open.

Rebecca was gone.

Chase pushed the door of Whip's cruiser open and stepped outside. As he stood, he saw the truck backing up in the yard. Rebecca was accelerating out of the yard toward the exit before Chase could clear the front of Whip's cruiser and make it to his own truck.

As Chase pulled out of the yard in pursuit, he glanced towards the door of the plant through his rearview mirror. His view was obstructed by both the ambulance and the helicopter and he briefly wondered if Whip was even aware of what was unfolding outside.

Chase moved to the rear of his vehicle until he could see down the front of the long hangar and the entrance to the airport from which he had come.

Nothing.

He advanced around the rear of his truck towards the tug.

Vacant.

He continued around the tug to Rebecca's truck.

Empty.

Chase ran unsteadily to the edge of the hangar and leaned against it. His ears picked up a low hum as he tentatively poked his head around it.

A sleek airplane lay idling on an expanse of concrete between the hangar and the airport's only runway. A slowly spinning turboprop was perched on each wing.

Rebecca was approaching the bottom of the stairs—or where the stairs would be if the plane's door was open. Chase needed to get to her before the door opened and the stairs came down.

Instead of the door opening to welcome Rebecca, the hum of the plane's engines increased in volume and pitch. Chase thought he could hear Rebecca's voice, but she was facing away from him, and whatever she said was overcome by the rhythmic, chopping sound of the propellers.

Rebecca reached out a hand as if it could stop that plane. Chase thought he heard her voice again, but it was unintelligible.

The propellers became a blur behind the throbbing roar of the turbines as the plane began to move.

Rebecca turned around. When she saw Chase, she began to run. Chase followed. They ran as the plane began accelerating down the runway.

Rebecca made it to the next building and inside the door.

Chase, aware of how unarmed he was, opened the door to the building cautiously. The door of the pilots' lounge was heavy. He tried to push it open and snake back to the edge of the doorway to inspect the inside of the room from relative cover. Instead, the pneumatic door closer on the commercial door resisted his effort and pushed the door closed again.

The sounds of the plane faded into the sky.

Chase was forced to lean into the door with all of his weight and found himself a step inside, with no cover, as he surveyed the room. There was no sign of Rebecca in the brightly lit space.

This was Chase's first time inside the pilots' lounge. Freshly remodeled, it looked more like a classroom than a lounge. Decorated in grays and whites, the modern furniture was clearly designed to be moved around to suit multiple uses. Along the back wall ran a length of countertop home to a coffee machine, cups, and some other mundane items. In the middle of it was the room's only other exit.

Chase navigated around the maze of separate tables.

Above the frosted glass door was a sign that read "Members Only." The frosting obscured the room beyond it, but the space did appear to be dark, much darker than the room he was in. Chase wrapped his right hand around the handle and pulled the door open with all of his might.

Unlike the commercial door at the entrance to the lounge, the interior door did not resist his effort. It swung open violently and crashed into the countertop, making no effort to retract to its closed position.

Chase, concealed by the doorframe, could only see into part of the next room. It was paneled in tongue and groove beadboard finished in an ebony stain. There were small pods of leather chairs, no different than those that sat in the Butterfield or

August's gun room, arranged for intimate conversations.

The room smelled of earth, cedar, and tobacco—the smells of a cigar lounge not an airport classroom. Chase edged closer into the room but was still unwilling to give up the safety of the doorframe. A bar shelf lined the back wall and held amber-, gold-, emerald-, and ruby-colored bottles. Chase silently chided himself for wasting time and finally stepped fully into the room.

He spoke into the darkness. "Rebecca."

"Have a seat," came a voice from his left. His eyes adjusted to find Rebecca standing in the darkest corner of the room. In her hand was a gun.

Chase raised his hands as he turned to face her. Behind her sat a bank of small wooden lockers. Humidors for cigars. Each had a label he couldn't make out from that distance.

Rebecca stood behind a waist-high bar. In front of her sat a small metal lockbox no bigger than a lunchbox. It was open, having likely already served its purpose of storing the handgun she now held.

She waved towards a leather chair with the barrel of the gun. Chase followed it and sat facing her. He allowed his arms and hands to relax on each armrest.

"Missed your ride?" Chase asked.

Silence.

"Baxter left you behind?"

More silence.

"Running from the cops was more than he could take?"

"No," Rebecca said. Her voice was steady, confident. "Baxter made the right choice. I have this under control."

"You killed Turner Cam," Chase said. "And tried to frame me for it."

She stared at him silently again.

"The key, Rebecca."

She took an audible breath. "I've never killed anyone."

"Baxter did?"

"No. Baxter is a good man." Her hand was steady. "A businessman."

"Brady Laye?" Chase knew this wasn't true. He wasn't even sure why he said it.

She raised an eyebrow theatrically but didn't speak.

He knew the name, and it wasn't Brady Laye. Brady was just a weak man trying to survive. A pawn.

He knew the name.

"Cody Bird," Chase said.

Her raised eyebrow relaxed. She straightened her posture. "He handed me the key. Like a child handing you an ugly piece of art they made. He was so proud."

"He got that key from his wife and then did the deed for you?"

"Who cares where he got the key?" Her eyes narrowed. "No one asked him to do it. Don't you get it? There's no confession, because there's nothing to confess."

"And Tacy?" Chase asked.

"You know all of this." She shook the barrel of the pistol at him. "Remember telling me that? You know all of this?"

"Turner Cam and Aaron Foster killed her to shut her up? Because they were stealing from the airport? And making sure your projects got approved?"

She didn't move much less reply.

"How did Cody know that the mayor had turned on you?"

"Everybody knew he couldn't be mayor again. Not after his meltdown. Not after he told you about Scout Commercial Partners."

Chase swallowed hard. Rebecca had removed any doubt. Chase's own lie had led to Turner Cam's murder.

37

Meet & Right

Chase's mind was struggling under the weight of the revelation that his own words really had led to Turner Cam's murder—not that anyone would miss him. Chase felt guilty anyway.

Properly guilty.

Chase was staring at the business end of a pistol for the third time that day. At least it wasn't his own gun this time.

"What's your plan considering Baxter didn't offer you a ride out of here?"

"I'm sure that the answer will walk through that door."

"The only thing coming though that door is Whip, and he'll be coming to arrest you."

"You still have a lot to learn about how things work out here."

Chase feared she was right.

"When Whip gets here," Rebecca continued, "we can talk about how you broke into my business and killed one of my employees because you heard a rumor that Cody Bird followed you to Castle Gap and took a shot at you. I couldn't have planned your destruction to be so complete."

"You did plan it."

"No, that's what makes it so great. I have no idea who shot at you, but it sure did provide an opportunity for someone to bait you into a fight—a fight that will finally get you thrown into jail where you belong."

As the words left her mouth, her eyes went to the door. "Sheriff! Thank God!"

Chase whipped around to see the sheriff in the doorway, pistol in his hand but pointed towards the floor at the ready.

"This man. He got out of the police car at the rendering plant. I was so scared. I ran for my life, and he chased me here. Look at the cars outside!" Rebecca set the pistol down as she spoke.

Chase's head was on a swivel. Whip behind him, Rebecca in front of him. He had run from the cops, too.

The young deputy entered behind Whip. He roughly pulled Chase from the chair, pushed him against the counter near Rebecca, and cuffed him. Whip joined him to secure Rebecca's firearm.

"I'm placing you under arrest for evading detention," the young deputy said. "You have the right to remain silent." He emptied Chase's back pockets. A wallet.

"Anything you say can and will be used against you in a court of law." He emptied Chase's right front pocket. A pocketknife.

"You have the right to an attorney. If you cannot afford an attorney, one will be provided for you." He emptied Chase's left front pocket. Car keys and a lone key—*the* key.

"Do you understand these rights as I have read them to you?" He searched Chase's other shirt pockets and removed one audio recorder—light glowing red.

Chase looked to Rebecca. Her cold eyes stared right back at him. Her lips formed a subtle, almost imperceptible smirk. She did not speak as Whip circled the bar and pulled her wrists behind her back. He led her out to the young deputy's cruiser and into the back seat—like a common criminal.

The young deputy walked Chase to Whip's cruiser and placed him in the back of it. Whip walked over and opened the door. Chase could hear the young deputy, who had walked over to Rebecca, read her Miranda rights. His voice disappeared as Whip sat down and closed the door.

Whip spoke to Chase while looking at him through the rearview mirror. "I should listen to this right now?" He held up the recorder.

"Yes," Chase said.

"I hope it goes better for you than the phone." Whip pressed play, fast-forwarded, pressed play, and continued until he finally heard their voices.

"he handed me the key"

"she caught them stealing from the airport"

"you planting this key on me"

When the tape caught up to Whip entering the room, he stopped it. "So"—he let out an audible breath—"Cody just thought he could move up in the world by killing Turner Cam for the Whiteys?"

"Looks like it," Chase said.

"And Tacy? She was killed to cover up, what, $150k in stolen airport money?"

"Plus whatever they got from the Whiteys for getting deals done."

"A crumb of respect from the Whitey family might have been all they got. Or their standing in the community was protected," Whip said. He looked over at the other cruiser before continuing, "In the end they might have just killed her to avoid jail time . . . people have killed for less." Whip looked back at Chase in the mirror. "I guess she doesn't know Max never hit record. That there's no video."

* * *

Diego, Stefan, and Corely—the official welcome party—were assembled on the front porch as August's SUV arrived. The variety of drinks between them was just a small sample of what waited inside. Sarah was the first to hop out of the vehicle, leaving the passenger door open as she stepped to the rear door. She opened it and busied herself out of sight of the group.

As August exited the vehicle, Sarah took a step back from the door. The foot of a crutch hit the ground first followed by a second. Eventually, two shoes followed, and out popped Max. He was finally home. Sarah looked up at the group with a grin as she walked alongside him. August flanked him on the other side. The group let him amble up the stairs, with August's help, before giving him a warm welcome.

"Do you regret following Chase to Girvin?" Corely asked. "Maybe just a little bit?" She let out a laugh.

"Nah, having the mayor of this place owe me one is probably a good thing," Max said.

"It was my idea anyway," August said. He put his hand on Max's shoulder as the corners of his mouth turned up. "Sorry about that."

"Doctor says you're good?" Stefan asked.

"We're working through some temporary nerve damage—neurapraxia," Max explained. "Should sort itself out."

He took a seat on the porch while the group rotated in and out of the hunting cabin with varying food and drink. Chase settled into the chair next to him. "August doesn't owe you one.

It's my fault. I should have told you I was going to Girvin to confront Cody Bird."

"Nah, the second I told August about Brady Laye he told me to get out there. We had your back."

"Figures," Chase said. "Maybe August should have told me *his* plan."

"Everyone was tiptoeing around you."

"Fair," Chase replied. The rest of the crowd had filed inside. Their conversation and laughter were a suddenly distant sound as the door closed. Chase stared out at the horizon. He then looked down at the glass in his hand. He tilted it forward until he caught his reflection in it. "Hmm," he muttered.

Max snapped him out of his momentary funk. "Earth to Chase. What's on your mind?"

"Cardamom," Chase half-whispered to himself.

"What?"

"Nothing. I went by the church today. Got me thinking."

"Oh?"

"Confession. I actually did it."

"In one of those little wooden booths the priest sits in? Do Lutherans have those?"

"No, I went to the pastor's office. I told him everything."

"Everything? And he didn't kick you out of there?" Max laughed.

"Nope." Chase flashed a brief smile that quickly faded. "It was . . . I dunno."

"What?"

"I had started thinking that maybe God had decided I wasn't good enough, because justice always seems to be out of reach."

"And now you have to do ten Hail Marys and everything's fixed?"

"No. It turns out none of us are good enough . . . and we don't have to be. Unconditional love. You don't have to earn it."

"And justice?"

"Well, maybe we can't expect that in this life. Imperfect world and all that."

"Yeah, well—"

Their conversation was interrupted by the door opening and August and Stefan stepping onto the porch.

"Not much of a party out here," Stefan said.

"August, you said that Chase got cleared to take office?" Max asked.

Chase answered, "Yeah, the state says they're ready to certify the election, but I wonder if I should bow out. How much more can this town take?" Chase eyed the ice rolling around in his empty glass as he turned it in his hand.

"It survived the whole city staff quitting, right?" Max asked, turning to Chase with a raised eyebrow.

"Yeah." Chase laughed. "Well, the public works guys just kept their heads down and filled potholes. Everything else is run by private contractors. The only thing that office staff did was look the other way on Aaron Foster's and Turner Cam's shenanigans."

"If you don't take office, you can't stop the airport deal. Right?" Stefan asked.

"That's the only thing Brady Laye was any good for. He was right about the mayor having the final say on that project. That's reason enough to take office," Chase said.

August took a seat next to Max and looked directly across at Chase as he spoke. "I had lunch with Whip today. Mostly asked him about Max, but you came up as well."

Stefan remained standing near the door.

"I'm still okay, right? That's what my lawyer says anyway," Max said.

"Whip says you are," Chase said.

"That's my read from him as well," August added.

Max looked to Chase. "*Bon camarade* and all that."

Chase smiled. "Yeah. You are a bona fide hero in my book."

"Twice." Max said as he shook two fingers at Chase. "I saved your life twice."

August tossed a folded newspaper over to Chase. "See this?"

Chase scrambled to catch the paper without dropping his glass. "Bad?"

"Nothing," August said.

"Really?"

"What are you guys on about?" Max asked. He snatched the paper from Chase.

"There's never been a word about any of this in the paper," August said.

"Like it never even happened," Chase said. He looked back to August. "Did Whip tell you the latest on Cody Bird and the Whiteys?"

"He's definitely not as open with the details with me as he is with you."

"What's the latest?" Stefan asked.

"The way I hear it, Cody Bird really didn't have any dirt on Rebecca or Baxter. Sounds like they are going to nail him for Turner Cam, though," Chase said.

"With Rebecca's help?" Max asked.

"She's probably sitting at the pilots' lounge with Baxter having a cocktail as we speak. Her little obstruction of justice and evading detention charges vanished the moment she flipped on Cody," Chase said.

"If Cody could connect the Whiteys to a murder he would. The fact is he can't. Whip says the guy acted alone. I believe him. Whip has always stuck his neck out for you," August said.

"Didn't feel like it sitting in his interviews—interrogations, really."

"And you walked away from all of those without any charges," August replied.

"And so did Rebecca Whitey," Chase said.

"In exchange for putting a real killer, Cody Bird, behind bars. Letting her go for framing you was the trade that had to happen," Stefan said.

"I know this," Chase said with a sigh.

"Then why do you look like you lost?" Stefan asked.

"I did lose." Chase looked past Max and August as he spoke. They looked down at the dry, cracked boards of the porch.

"You won," said Stefan. "Aaron Foster and Turner Cam are dead. They acted alone. You can take office and kill the Whiteys' airport project right at the finish line. They deserve it. Then you can make sure nothing like it ever comes up again. You can end the handouts to the Whiteys and their backroom deals."

"I lost"—Chase looked up at Stefan—"the only thing that actually mattered."

He swallowed to avoid saying her name.

www.ingramcontent.com/pod-product-compliance
Ingram Content Group UK Ltd.
Pitfield, Milton Keynes, MK11 3LW, UK
UKHW040159231025
464254UK00004B/184

9 798998 522017